# IN THE SWEEP OF THE BAY

# IN THE SWEEP OF THE BAY

## Cath Barton

**2020**
Louise Walters Books

A catalogue card for this book is available from the British Library.

Produced and published in 2020
by Louise Walters Books

ISBN 9781999630577
eISBN 9781999630584

Typeset in PTSerif 11.5pt by Blot Publishing: www.blot.co.uk

Printed and bound by Clays Ltd, Elcograf S.p.A

louisewaltersbooks.co.uk

info@louisewaltersbooks.co.uk

Louise Walters Books
PO Box 755
Banbury
OX16 6PJ

# ABOUT THE AUTHOR

Cath Barton won the New Welsh Writing Ameri-Cymru Prize for the Novella 2017 for *The Plankton Collector*. Her short stories and flash fiction have been published in anthologies in the UK, the US and Australia, and in journals including The Lonely Crowd, Strix, Fictive Dream, The Cabinet of Heed, After the Pause and Spelk. Born in the English Midlands, she now lives in Abergavenny, South Wales.

The mass of men live lives of quiet desperation

*Henry David Thoreau (1817-1862)*

Bring me sunshine in your smile,
Bring me laughter all the while,
In this world where we live
there should be more happiness,
So much joy you can give
to each brand new bright tomorrow,
Make me happy through the years
never bring me any tears,
Let your arms be as warm
as the sun from up above,
Bring me fun, bring me sunshine, bring me love!

*Arthur Kent and Sylvia Dee (1966)*

# 2009

When they put up the statue in 1999, they advertised for someone to look after it. I've been a street sweeper all my life, got all the qualifications, so I knew I had a good chance. It's a part-time job, which suits me fine. Some folk say the Brits are lazy, but it's not true up here. Good workers, the men of Lancashire, always have been. But there comes a time when you want to spend a bit more of the day with your feet up. Over seventy years of age – no, I don't look it, I know, people are always saying – it's reasonable, don't you think? But there's only me at home now and looking at the four walls all day drives you up them. So I'm glad of the job. Bit of extra on top of my pension comes in handy, too. I have holidays in places I never dreamt I'd go. Canada I went to last year. Those Rocky Mountains, wow! Though our Lakeland Fells are just as beautiful, in my opinion, just not quite as high, and they're right in my line of vision every day, out there on the other side of the bay. Marvellous.

When people look at me and say, How could you do that job? I tell them about my view. I meet people from all over the world. This statue I look after, it's the most photographed sight in the world, straight up! You google it if you don't believe me. Folk come from New Zealand. They've got big mountains there where they filmed *Lord of the Rings*, but according to what I understand they played about with them, man-ip-u-lated them into something they're not for those films. They wouldn't have had to do that if they'd chosen our mountains here in England. Anyway, as I was saying, people come from the four corners. I've had people from Fiji, Shangri-la, Timbuktu, you name it.

Amazing! That's what they all say about our Eric here. That he is amazing and that the statue is just like him. It's what brings them so far. After all, they've all got statues where they come from. He is, I will grant you, slightly bigger than life-size, but so realistic. The posture! On one leg, dancing like he did with Ern at the end of their TV shows. Marvellous. The bloke that made it, he's a genius. Got our Eric to a tee, what a fellow. Course, you might not know this so I'll tell you, he wasn't born with the name Morecambe. No sir. Born here though and took the name of the town. Straight up. Bet you didn't know that, not everyone does. I enjoy a little chat with folk, breaks up the day. Offer to take their photograph too. They often appreciate that. Gives them a souvenir of their day out. That can mean a lot to folk, especially when they're older.

Sometimes I come along and find that one of the ruddy gulls has shat on his head! Honestly – they don't care. Steal chips off old ladies they do. And off children, those great beaks they have frighten the little bastards. But to do their business on Eric's head, sacrilege I call it. I have some special stuff I use to keep Eric spick and span for his visitors. That gets it off. Council issue, you can't get it in the shops, works a treat. That's my first job every morning. Give Mr M's head a good wipedown with my special stuff. I work down from there. All the way down to his shoes. Rub-a-dub-dub with the shoe-shine cloth and he's done.

Then I sweep the steps. One thing that people do – can you believe this? – they only drop their chewing gum on the steps! I ask you. What a mess, and a person could slip. I use the special Council stuff on that too. Cleanest steps in Lancashire though I say so myself. People appreciate it. And they do like a chat, if they understand English that is, not all of them do. But there's lots of folk only too glad to pass the time of day. Chaps on their own specially. Often lost their wives, like me. Some say how nice it would be to find a little job like this where they live. Mornings only. Home in time for lunch, though I treat myself in a café on Fridays. Fish I have.

There are that many people I meet, that many stories I hear, I could write a book. People think my job is menial, sweeping steps sounds like it is, don't it? – but there is a lot more to it than that. You have to be, how shall I put it, you have to be *sensitive* to people. Know when they want to talk and when they want to be left alone. I don't rush in.

There was this couple, in their late sixties, I suppose they were. And a bit awkward with one another, like people get when they've been busy with jobs and family responsibilities and then, hey presto, retirement strikes, they're together all day and every day and they find they have to get to know each other all over again and it's not so easy. They didn't live far away, these two, came on the bus they told me, had their lunch in the place I like. Good fish there, lovely and fresh. There was something about them, I couldn't say what it was. Like a shadow they both had behind them. Hark at me, talking like some kind of ologist! But you know, straight up, my heart went out to the pair of them and it felt like me taking their picture wasn't just run of the mill but something that mattered. It stayed with me, that feeling I got from them. Not that I suppose for one minute they're the only ones like that. Goodness knows happiness is not divvied up fairly in this life, is it? Though there was another couple that same day, earlier on, the exact opposite. Two chaps, gay couple they looked like, one of them a foreigner. I can't be doing with people that start up with comments about either gays or foreigners. The good Lord put us all together on the earth, is what I say. They wanted to give me money to take their photo. As if, I said to them. It is my pleasure, I said.

Must have been about five years ago I reckon, if my memory serves me right. And today, this happens. First, there's the sad woman again, on her own, and her eyes are red and I know her hubby's gone and that, in spite of everything, she's missing him. She doesn't come up to me, she skirts around and goes a little way off and stands and looks out over the bay. I remember them doing that together. It could break my heart, what life and death does to folk. I don't think I'll see her again. People often follow quickly, when they've been together a long time. However it's been for them.

Then, not long after, the foreign bloke. And he comes straight up to me, big smile on his face, and says, Hello, how are you? Holds out his hand to shake mine and offers me a fag. I've given up, but how nice is that? Thank you, but no thank you I say, you're a gent, and he laughs and says not many people say that. I ask him where he's from and he says Italy and he's working in the Midland Hotel. And I ask what happened to his friend and he says, You've got a good memory, he lives in London but he comes up here for *Strictly* in Blackpool, funnily enough that's next weekend, he says, and he tells me his friend Sandra has got tickets for him and his new boyfriend to go and see it. I say I've never watched but I'm going to take a look now. Look out for me on the TV, he says as he goes off. Nice fella. People are something else; they open your eyes to things you've not thought of, they really do.

So strange, seeing those people again, on the same day. Some people say there's no such thing as coincidence. I don't know. I'm just an ordinary chap.

# 1984

The gulls sitting on the freshly-painted blue railings flap into the morning sky as one, before peeling off on their individual journeys across the bay, riding the thermals here, swooping down on abandoned chip papers there. On this day of midwinter-spring the bay is theirs, from the Lakeland Fells under their snow duvet down past where, one day in the future, a statue of Eric Morecambe will be forever dancing and the curve of the Midland Hotel will shine bright white once more, to the estuary that divides Lancashire from the country south. Towards which cars and trains trundle on the twin skeins of motorway and railway which lie on the land like wool on a giant's knitting needles. The gulls know their territory. They stay within the sweep of Morecambe Bay.

Below them, land-bound, the lives of the people of the bay move, intertwining now and then, into this new day. It is a day never before known and yet, for many, one that will follow well-worn, familiar patterns. Though not for all. Not for Ted Marshall, surprised by a sudden sharp pain that made him double up before his shaving mirror, so that he is now in an ambulance speeding with sirens to hospital.

Nor, in equal but different measure, for Irene – Rene – Ted's wife of thirty years, twisting a handkerchief as the ambulance carries Ted away from her, maybe for ever, leaving her at home alone regretting her harsh words of the morning and thinking Ted much too young to die. Rene does not know – how could she? – that the road will be clear, the queue short, and so the doctors will, on this occasion, save him. And that this will also save their marriage, giving them cause to take stock and start small moves back towards one another. And all the time, above the bay, the gulls make their laughing cries.

New-minted this day, too, for a young couple who watch the gulls take off from their blue line, a couple on their honeymoon. The magic of their relationship is as fresh and bright as the paint on the railings, which they admire with their love-shiny eyes as they stand side by side looking out over the sheen and the sweep of the bay. She takes a photograph of him standing next to a statue of a gull on a plinth, a gull so much larger than life-size. They laugh together about this and he pulls his new wife to him.

'I'll never take you for granted,' he says, gazing into her limpid eyes.

It is a promise as solemn and important as the wedding vows so recently exchanged. They had walked up the daffodil path to the church separately and back down it together, and that yellow flower will always be especially theirs. That's what she says to him now, with her diffident, ever-endearing laugh.

The bus on which Rene is travelling north to be with Ted in hospital, and another on which the young couple are heading south to look at the Viking graves at Heysham, stop on opposite sides of the road at the same village bus stop. For a moment the young woman's eyes meet Rene's through the murky windows and there is a silent exchange. Neither of them could put into words what passes between them in that moment, but it stirs them both. The newly-married woman does not mention this to her husband, who is pulling at her sleeve, pointing out a small object of delight. She makes a movement of her shoulders, not a shrug exactly, but a sloughing off of future grief, for that is what she has seen in Rene's eyes. This, though, is a promise-of-spring day, and Ted is going to live. Rene has as much reason as the young woman to rejoice, did she but know it, but for now fear is fluttering at her back.

The young couple are amazed by the Viking graves, the hollowing-out of the solid stone. They wonder how on earth people did that, so long ago. He takes her left hand, squeezes it, feels the ring on her finger and swells with pride. His wife. He has an impulse to rush her back to the flat they have rented for the week. But he resists, thinking there will be not just today, but all the days of their lives for shared passion. He does not know how it will really be, any more than Ted knew when he was twenty and married Rene. When he too thought they would have all the days of their lives.

All through the slow greying of the afternoon Rene sits by Ted's bedside in the hospital ward as he dozes and the nurses go to and fro. In the evening the gulls return to their roosting places on the shore. Ted will stay in the hospital tonight. He tells Rene he is tired. She, taking it as a dismissal, travels home on the bus, sitting on the upper deck so that she can look out across the now dark but still shining and calming sweep of the bay.

When she gets back to the house where she has lived with her husband since the day they were married, Rene does not, for once, look at the shabby corners and sigh. She pulls open the wide drawer, the one that sticks, at the bottom of the sideboard and takes out the book of their wedding photographs. She wants, urgently, to see the expressions on their twenty-year-old faces on that spring day. It is as she thought. They are veiled in shyness, but there is unquestionably the looking forward, side by side. It is what she saw from the bus in the face of the young woman, obscured by the dirt on the bus window, but still clearly unquashable.

In their holiday flat the honeymoon couple lie entwined, listening to the sweet susurration of the sea. If she were to see her again, Rene would not go past without telling that young woman to treasure her marriage, to hold it always in her hands as carefully as she would a fragile flower. As regrets swirl in her mind she thinks of Ted, lying alone in the hospital bed, and feels a long-closed door in her heart begin to creak open. Rene knows, with sudden and simple clarity, what to do. While the kettle is boiling for her tea, she finds what she needs. Anyone passing the house on the evening of this day will, if they stop for a moment and listen, hear the urgent clack-clack of Rene's knitting needles. She is knitting for Ted. The work will occupy her hands, and still the agitation of her mind, until weariness brings her the benediction of sleep.

And all the while, up and down the lines of railway and motorway that weave and spool, as the wool does at Rene's feet, the trains and cars travel on into the night.

# THE FIFTIES

Ted had not had choices. Not when he was young. Leaving school at fifteen and starting work in the family firm had always been a certainty. He hadn't questioned it, any more than he'd questioned day following night. He'd done his apprenticeship like everyone else. It made no difference that he was a member of the family, he needed to learn the same as others did. His Aunt Lavinia was the head of the firm in the fifties. She was respected by the workers as much as any man. They'd started him on sugar basins. The feel of the clay slipping under his fingers on the wheel had quickly become second nature to him. He had, his Aunt Lavinia used to say proudly, the Family Feel.

Three years' apprenticeship and Ted moved to the painting benches. This was long before he designed the first Edward Marshall vase, of course, but it was clear to his workmates from the start that painting was to be his métier. Ted was happy. He spent his evenings listening to plays on the radio as he experimented with new designs for the factory. Except on Fridays. Friday night was music night on the *Light Programme* and Ted tapped his feet to the big bands as he worked.

'You could go to the Palais now you're eighteen,' Ted's mother said to him one day. 'Why don't you try it?'

Ted wasn't sure. Working with his hands was something he was easy with; talking wasn't, especially talking to girls. He went to the Palais, but only to please his mother. The boys stood on one side of the ballroom and the girls on the other. Ted had no idea what to do, the room was so grand and the girls so unknown, so he bought a ginger beer and sat listening to the band as couples formed and reformed. He loved it when players stood up and lifted their instruments for a solo. He could have watched them all night. And would have done if there hadn't been a Ladies' Excuse Me.

Some of the boys acted cocky as the girls sashayed across the room to take their pick. Ted was terrified. What if he was chosen? What if he wasn't? His first dance was with a hefty girl called Judith who must have eaten spring onions in her dinner. Ted's sister always picked out the onions, if

14

they had them, on dance night. Now he knew why. Judith was not a girl who waited to be told what to do. She shoved him into place and hissed the steps into his ear. It was terrible. When Judith broke away at the end of their dance another girl was there, smiling at him.

'She's a bit much, our Judith. Don't take on, it's really not your fault.'

Ted didn't know what to say, but he heard the invitation coming out of his mouth as if there was some magical ventriloquist working him. And she was saying yes, please with her head inclined all coy and next thing they were dancing. Her name was Irene she said, everyone calls me Rene, you must too, and she wasn't really friends with Judith so he wasn't to worry himself. Rene was to Ted, from that very first dance, inevitable. He had no more choice than he'd had about working at the factory.

The next week, when Friday came, his mother asked him if he'd be going to the Palais and he found himself saying he would be, even though he hadn't really thought about it. Rene was outside waiting for him as if they'd been courting for months. Later he wondered about the week before, whether she'd had her eye on him all evening. Not that she was bad-looking. There were other boys who asked her to dance, but she told them she was spoken for. Deep down inside Ted there was a little voice that tried to protest, to say it would be good to stand and watch a little longer, just stand and listen to the band. But either he didn't hear the voice or he pushed it away. It came to him again years later, that voice, when he thought about the what ifs.

At the end of the evening Ted and Rene walked along the front, as the lights winked around the bay, and did what all young couples did to a greater or lesser extent, his arm around her waist pulling her in for a goodnight kiss. And another. But, in their case, no further. Ted didn't know how and Rene was scared of babies.

'*About* babies,' she corrected herself. 'When we're married it'll be different,' she said, all coy again.

So, in a way, it was she who proposed. Or rather it was assumed, by everyone, that Ted and Rene would marry. They courted for two years and then, sure enough, they were wed, the year after rationing for sweet things had ended. Even though meat would still be on the ration for another couple of months, his mother got hold of all sorts and put on a wonderful spread, such as they hadn't seen for years. The wedding was in May. Rene had lilac in her bouquet, which was a funny choice, rather heavy, and by the time they had the pictures taken it was drooping. Rene took against the scent of lilac from that day forward.

*

There was a day, before the children were born. A carefree day. It was strange that neither of them talked about it, later, and a pity there was no one to remind them. If there had been it might have helped. A reminder of happiness to ease the sorrowful times.

They were settling into their respective roles of provider and housewife. The summer had flowered early and withered by late August, but in the last week of September there came an unexpectedly fine day. Ted, acting on a rare impulse, sent a message to the factory that he would not be able to come in. He felt, for once in his life, no guilt.

'Come on, love,' he said to Rene, pulling on the ties of her apron, lifting it over her head and turning her to him. 'We'll go out. We'll go to the Fells.'

Rene, caught off-guard, did a little jump of genuine delight. 'I'll cut sandwiches,' she said.

And she did. They went on their bikes across to the bay and north, the sea to their left sparkling like sapphires. Ted could have sworn he saw a dolphin leaping, out of the corner of his eye. He told Rene and they laughed about it. Oh, how they laughed together that day. If only, Rene said, they could have bottled some of that laughter. She'd have kept it in the kitchen cupboard like a bottle of the most expensive spirits, to bring out and sniff if ever times got hard. Though on that day the future looked to them both as sunny as the weather.

With the wind at their backs the bikes seemed to fly north. They went further than anyone would have thought possible. They crossed the river Kent with the bulk of Sizergh Castle to the north, and soon they were on the long straight road called Lord's Plain Causeway that took them to the foot of Cartmel Fell. And there was just the place to leave their bikes, with a shop, a miraculous find in such remote parts. Ted went in for chocolate.

'A treat!' he declared, breaking off two pieces for them right away. The fresh air and the miles travelled would make it all the tastier, he told Rene.

The day shone upon them as they strode up the hill. It seemed no time before they were high up and looking down on Lake Windermere. Rene gasped at its beauty. She had never known there was this, so close to home. The Lakeland Fells had, until that day, been for her the hills across the bay. Lovely to look at from a distance, yes, but not a place she would ever, could ever, visit.

They stopped to eat their sandwiches at a place where the whole world, or so it seemed, was set out at their feet: the Old Man of Coniston to the west, Helvellyn to the north, the green, grassy slopes of the Howgills to the east; and, far away south across the bay, tiny but clear, the outline of Blackpool Tower. Ted turned to his young wife and slid an arm around her waist, just as he had on the day they first met, but confident now.

'I love you,' he said.

Rene blushed. 'And I you.'

Don't forget, they said to one another. But whether it was because of the dreamlike quality of the day, the stillness of the air, the loud birdsong or the distance from home – so near and yet so far – it would slip from them, this magic they had tasted.

At the end of the day they cycled home. The sea, on their right now, was midnight blue with a line of plankton phosphorescence on the shore. Replete with the day's joys, they drank cocoa and fell into bed and, immediately, sleep.

The next day it was as if none of this had happened. The morning was grey. Ted went to the factory and Rene to her round of housewifely chores. At tea-time they quarrelled over something small, Ted went out to the pub and Rene sat in the kitchen mending something. Socks, probably. There were always socks in need of mending.

They forgot the happiness. Or rather, they pushed it away. But it was there, all their lives, waiting to surprise them. Now and again it did. An unexpected smile from one to the other could do it, or Rene putting her arm through Ted's on a bus ride and him letting her.

After they had both died their daughters could see it, that tracery of happiness, in some of the old photos, flickering on the pictures as if they were lantern slides. That made it easier, somehow, to bear their passing, and to carry on themselves, knowing that happiness was always only a memory away.

# THE SIXTIES

They were grand days for Ted, the sixties. Though when he looked back later, he could see it differently, could see that those days maybe weren't so grand for his wife. Definitely not, he had to admit. Her at home with two little girls. Their darling girls, no question about that. They both loved them so much. Peg and Dot. Margaret and Dorothy, they were christened, but they liked the short names. Rene's mother tut-tutted.

'We christened you Irene, and that's your name in God's eyes,' she said. 'Same with your girls. And as for your husband—'

'Shush, Mother, Ted's a good man.'

The girls loved their dad. They took it in turns to ride on Ted's back in the garden; he was the horse. They couldn't have afforded riding lessons, but if the girls hankered after anything like that they never said. Happy to play at home. Simple pleasures they had, back then. Ted enjoyed those times with his girls. He didn't stop to think about Rene, who most likely was in the kitchen, getting tea for all of them.

Peg's sixth birthday fell on a Sunday, so they were round the table for tea, the four of them. Rene had made egg and cress sandwiches, which both the children loved, though Ted fussed about the cress.

'You know I like plain food, Mum,' he said.

'You won't know unless you try, Dad,' said Peg. 'Mum makes the best sandwiches.'

She was an adventurous child when it came to food, more so than her sister. She was willing to take risks in every way when she was young. Her drawings were big and bold and colourful; Dot drew small figures in the corners of the paper. Peg jumped into the water straightaway the first time Rene took the children to a swimming pool, while Dot stood hugging herself with her toes curling over the edge. Things would be different when they grew up, Dot taking more of the chances with life, though the two of them would always be close.

For now, everything was about the day. Rene had started going to continental cookery classes and had made special biscuits, sandwiched with butter cream and her homemade raspberry jam, with one end dipped in chocolate.

'They're called Viennese fingers,' she said proudly.

Even Ted ate one and seemed to enjoy it, and as Peg was blowing out the candles on the cake her mother had baked, Rene smiled across the table at her husband through the shimmer and he smiled back.

'Well done, Mum,' he said, patting her shoulder as he got up from the table, and she basked in the praise; though that night, when they went to bed, his kiss was perfunctory before he turned away onto his side as usual, and she felt sad.

Rene did believe though, in the sixties, that it was her place to be at home, keeping house. She was proud of her husband. He was doing well at the factory. He was very clean, never had paint on his hands when he came home. And he never came home the worse for drink. She appreciated those things. There were other men – she didn't know who or what they did exactly, just heard tut-tutting in the shops in town – but she knew she was lucky with Ted. She told herself that, when she felt tired. In the evenings when the children were in bed and Ted was reading a book and she was still in the kitchen, preparing his sandwiches for the next day. Every day.

She kept a good house. And she made sure her husband and her two girls always had clean outer and underwear. She knew cleanliness was important. Her own mother had always said so. And she'd never questioned her mother. Except she wouldn't have her saying anything against Ted. He was a good man. And one day, she told her mother, Ted would be famous for his work, he'd have his own designs, and yes, then he would use his full name, and vases with the name Edward Marshall on them would be in all the big shops in London. Rene had no idea whether this would happen. She said it to shut her mother up, because her mother was a snob. She was surprised at herself, making up a story. She really didn't know much about Ted's work at the factory. She would have liked to, but it wasn't the thing to ask a man about his work. Or how much he earned. The fact was he'd bought them a house and he gave her housekeeping money every week. She had nothing to complain about. That was what she thought. Though she was so tired, some nights she couldn't sleep, and that was when fears and questions began to spiral in her mind. But she pushed them away, because she truly believed that Ted was a good man.

Ted did not question things. It was not his way. He went to work at the factory from Monday to Friday. He enjoyed his work. There were men he knew who did not enjoy their work. But not at S & L Marshall.

They made the finest ceramics in Lancashire; Aunt Lavinia had always said so. Ted was proud to work in the family firm. Proud to be trusted with painting Aunt Lavinia's most detailed designs now. Proud to have an assistant of his own, a girl starting work at the factory at the age of fifteen, as he had. Madge Turner was a quiet girl, and neat. He liked that, her being so contained. It was companionable, working alongside each other at the green baize workbench. She'd fetch the vases after their first firing, lay out the paints and the brushes, change his water. She got to know the pace of the work; he knew he could rely on her. They didn't talk much. Ted liked the quiet, but now and then he'd have an urge to hear some music.

'Let's have Music While You Work on, Madge,' he'd say.

And she'd turn on the wireless and they'd hum along to the tunes they knew. Sometimes they'd find themselves singing the words together. There was a song they both liked called 'Bring Me Sunshine'. It made Madge smile, and Ted found himself thinking of the lovely smile she had, thinking about her when he was in bed, before he went to sleep. But he felt guilty about that. He had a wife, a good wife, and he knew he should be content. It troubled him that he was stirred at all by another woman, and her only a few years older than his own daughters.

Ted knew his mother-in-law looked down on him for working with his hands, and he was grateful that Rene always stuck up for him. She really was a brick, back in those years. Later, when time had started to wear them down, he wished he'd told her earlier how much he appreciated her. He could see that they could have talked more, that it might have helped, but she was always so busy, and worn out by the end of the day. She tossed and turned in the night, and she didn't mean to, he knew, but it kept him awake and he suggested having separate beds. It was only to help them both get a good night's sleep, he said. He still loved her. Perhaps, he thought later, he should have said that too. But men didn't, not after their courting days. Not then, anyway.

By the end of the decade the factory was indeed producing, alongside those vases in the Lavinia Marshall Traditions catalogue, a new range – Edward Marshall Ware. He used floral designs, but in his own distinctive way, and signed each vase with his initials, EM, in a cursive script. There were people who came to the factory: buyers, ceramics experts, people who wrote about Ted's designs in the trade press. They used words like Modernist, Innovative and Daring. Ted was amused – he drew the flowers that grew in his garden, the garden that Rene cultivated.

One day a different kind of woman arrived with an appointment to see Ted. She'd come up from London for the day, complete with red high heels, a bobbed haircut and dark glasses. Whispers went around that she was from a fashion magazine.

'Don't be daft, lass,' Ted said to Madge when she told him what people were saying. 'We make pots, not frocks.'

But it was true. The woman had a photographer in tow, and there were Edward Marshall vases in the next issue of *Vogue*, and a picture of Ted and his "charming" assistant.

'Don't we look a lovely couple?' he said to her. And she blushed. But then, Madge always blushed easily.

That was the closest it ever came.

There were times when Ted tried to talk to his wife about his designs, times when they began conversations even. But she always seemed to be busy with one thing or another, her mind elsewhere. Sometimes at weekends, especially in the summer, he would take a drawing pad into the garden. He'd sit in a deckchair, sketching, while Rene worked on her hands and knees, weeding amongst the roses and the delphiniums and the cornflowers.

'Come and take a look, love,' he'd say.

And she'd get up, wiping the earth from her hands in an impatient sort of way, and look over his shoulder at his drawings. But she never lingered, never sat down beside him.

'I've so much to do,' she'd say.

And it was true, there was a lot to do; they had a big garden.

There was a day, clear in his memory, when Ted held out his hand to his wife, was about to ask her to stop, even to pull her onto his knee, to embrace her there and then, just as he had when they were courting, but she said she had to get the tea and he felt it as a slap, and it widened the space between them, as did every little thing like that.

After that he stopped showing her his drawings, showed them first to Madge at the factory. Madge was always appreciative. Of course. It was her job to be. He knew that, but he felt she had a sympathy for the work that Rene would never have. And he felt guilty for feeling that. He pushed the feelings down, he had to; there was no one else he could talk to even if he'd ever thought of doing so, which he hadn't. Because men didn't.

# THE SEVENTIES

Rene didn't ask Ted much about his work. Just whether he'd had a good day. To which he generally replied that he had, because he loved his work.

'I think you love your work more than you love me, Ted,' Rene used to say. She said it with a smile in the early days, as a joke. But as time went on and distance widened between them, she smiled less often.

Ted didn't love his work more than he loved his wife, but he spent more time at the factory than he did with her, and when he got home at night he was tired and ready for his meal. Often he would fall asleep in his chair soon afterwards, his newspaper crumpling on his knee, and Rene would go into the kitchen so as not to disturb him. She believed it was her place. When discontent rumbled inside her, she pushed it down.

'Ted has his job, and I have mine,' she said to the vicar, who came to call sometimes, concerned about all the women like Rene he saw in the shops of his parish. They rarely came to his church, but he understood that. He couldn't do anything to change matters; the mores of the time were bigger than him. But he did his bit.

'You must find something that is for you,' he said to Rene. 'Something beyond the house.' But he knew it was no simple matter. Rene, like the other women he visited, was thin and pale, worn by the work of a housewife, the dedication. She didn't tell him about the continental cookery classes. She'd given them up after Peg's last birthday party; they seemed like an indulgence, not something she should expect for herself. Ted was picky about his food anyway and Rene had been brought up not to waste anything.

'You should be like Mole in The Wind in the Willows,' the vicar said to her one blustery spring day. 'Throw down your duster and say, "Hang spring cleaning!" and just go out.'

'And where would I go?' said Rene.

To which the vicar had no answer, even though he would have liked to say, Come with me!

He prayed about his temptations, which were many and frequent. They were, he knew, his cross to bear. And Rene, mercifully oblivious to that, carried on with the housework and the putting of meals on the table for her husband and her children.

There were everyday ranges, tea sets mainly, which were produced in the factory, the bread and butter of the business. They had a production line, with its own supervisor, a man who Ted trusted completely. All he had to do was check with him once a week and everything went on as it needed to. Then there were the hand-painted pieces, vases mainly, which Ted designed and painted with the help of two apprentices. And Madge, of course, his personal assistant.

The apprentices started by hand-painting tiles, rows of which were commissioned for a number of municipal buildings in the town. Madge was skilled at the tile-painting, and she instructed the new apprentices. They were usually boys fresh from school, keen to learn and progress. There was plenty of work in the pottery industry in the sixties and even in the early seventies, when Hornsea opened a second factory in Lancaster. But it was a short-lived prosperity. The coalfields were closing, and in 1974 came the three-day week. Some factories struggled, but Ted Marshall was an astute businessman as well as a skilled craftsman, and he had the backing of other sensible people on his Board.

'Don't despair, lads – and lasses,' Ted said when he had to tell the workforce. 'It's dark days we're facing now, but we'll get through them, so long as we all remember we're a team.'

There was no denying that the workers experienced hardship that winter. But in the Marshall household there was still hot food on the table every night, for Rene had always been thrifty, and she made a little meat go a long way.

'You're a grand housewife,' Ted said to her as she dished up shepherd's pie or macaroni cheese. And, with him being home more than usual, they spent more time together that winter than for years before or after. The girls were teenagers by this time, out at the youth club on Saturday nights.

'We should go out again, Mum,' Ted said.

'But I've nowt to wear,' said Rene.

'Come on, now,' he said, pulling out a pound note and giving it to her. 'Buy some material and make yourself a skirt you can twirl in.'

That spring, when the three-day week was over and the daffodils announced that hope was real, Rene bought three yards of checked gingham in the market and made herself a gathered skirt and a blouse to go with it. She put them on and twirled for Ted and, in the space between their two beds and the dressing table, they danced cheek to cheek. And once, just once that year, they did go out, back to the Palais. But the ballroom had cracks in the walls, the band played pop tunes, and all the other dancers were young things who were just a year or two older than their own girls, so they left early and walked along the prom arm in arm. On the bus home Ted put his arm round his wife's shoulders and she leaned in to him.

'We're all right, love, aren't we?' he said.

And she nodded. But next day the weather turned, and the everyday round of work ambushed them both again.

There were, in other places at that time, stirrings amongst women. Rene knew nothing of that movement. She did not know how to satisfy the unnamed needs she felt within her, so she suppressed them. And Ted, poor Ted, did not know how to reach the woman he had fallen in love with and still loved, in his own way. So he stopped trying.

They came through that hard winter of 1974 and, for a while, things looked up. Ted designed a special vase that he gave to Rene for their twentieth wedding anniversary, though his pleasure was dented when he overheard her saying to another woman at the party that it was one more thing to dust. He pretended he hadn't heard, but something hardened inside him that day, like a part of his heart muscle dying. And maybe it did. But he still kissed his wife and said how lovely she looked, even as she glowered at Madge. Poor Madge who had no new frock and what had she done wrong anyway?

There'd been a letter. Rene couldn't believe it. Burned it. The phone call came soon after, one afternoon when she had her hands in flour, making scones for tea. She wiped them on her apron as she walked to the telephone. It was in the hall, by the front door. A draughty place, but in those days telephones were not for long conversations, they were for messages. As Rene picked up the receiver she noticed flour on the carpet and thought she must clean it up before the girls got home from school.

'Hello, Poulton 4672,' she said.

'Mrs Marshall?' said the voice on the other end. 'Am I speaking to Mrs Irene Marshall?'

Rene frowned. She was not expecting anyone to call. She did not recognise the voice. She needed to get on with her baking. 'Yes,' she said. 'Who is asking for her?'

'You don't need to know my name. This is just a friendly call.'

Rene felt her heart thumping. She didn't know what to say and just stood there, holding the receiver to her ear, looking down at the speckling of flour on the paisley-pattern of the carpet.

'Are you still there, Mrs Marshall?' There was a hiss on the line, or possibly in the voice.

'What do you want?' Her question came out more loudly than she intended.

'No need to shout now, Mrs Marshall. I'm just trying to be helpful.'

'Look, is this some kind of joke?' She wondered for a minute if it was one of the children putting on a voice.

'This is no laughing matter, Mrs Marshall. Just ask your husband.'

'Ask my husband?' Rene felt a shiver down her arms. The draught from the door. Or the woman's insinuating voice.

'Ask him about Miss Turner.'

'What? Hello? What are you saying?'

Silence at the other end. A click. The dialling tone.

Rene stumbled back into the kitchen, went to the sink and filled a glass with water from the cold tap. She sat on the kitchen stool with the red vinyl top and gulped down the water between great sobs. In a daze she drained the glass, washed her hands and picked up where she had left off making the scones. At four o'clock the girls were home. Rene gave them their tea. At six o'clock Ted was home from the factory. Rene gave him his tea. None of them appeared to notice anything, though Peg said:

'Scones were a bit flat today, Mum.'

'They were very nice,' said Ted. 'Don't cheek your mother.' But when he looked towards Rene, ready to give her a smile, she had already turned towards the kitchen. And none of them saw the tears in her eyes.

That night Rene was in bed before Ted had got upstairs.

'Rene, love,' he said quietly. But there was no answer. Rene lay with her face to the wall, eyes open, her mind snagging on the questions she dared not ask.

The next day, and the next, life went on as usual, except Rene was on edge, alert for the phone to ring. On the Friday she ran to its trilling.

'Yes?' Her voice was, she knew, sharp.

'Everything alright with you, Mrs Marshall?' It was the butcher, wondering if she still wanted the liver she had ordered but forgotten to collect.

'Yes, yes, of course. I'm sorry.'

It was a long time before Rene stopped jumping every time the phone rang. She said nothing to Ted about the letter or the anonymous caller but, tormented by her imaginings, began taking a longer walk to the shops, by a route that took her past the end of the road on which the factory of S & L Marshall stood, a dark mass at the top of the hill silhou-etted against the skyline. Her children ate lunch at school and her husband had his at the factory. But people did come out of the factory gates at one o'clock, when the siren rang for the men and women to lay down their tools, and Rene stood looking into the window of the shop opposite the end of the road, watching the reflections of the workers coming down the hill.

She had not planned what she would do if she saw Ted and Madge. She had seen them in her night-time imaginings, seen them walking arm in arm down the hill together, pausing, turning, smiling and moving closer. But she stopped short of allow-ing herself to see them kissing. It was too terrible.

Rene never saw her husband and his assistant together outside the factory. There was an occa-sion, during that period immediately following the anonymous telephone call, when she had to go there with an urgent letter for the business that – she didn't know why – had arrived at their home. Madge had come to the reception desk.

'Thank you, Mrs Marshall.'

That was all she said, and she kept her head inclined. Like all the workers she wore an overall, and a scarf over her head. It was the first time Rene had met Madge; she thought her a very plain girl. That, she knew, should have reassured her. But it did not. That night she tortured herself with thoughts of Madge taking off her anonymising overall and headscarf and pouting as she put on bright red lipstick. Then undoing the top button of her blouse. Then turning to Ted. Then. Rene turned over in bed and made herself think about what she would cook for tea the next day.

But then there was the coat. It was in the window of Shirley's dress shop. It was red and it had a fur collar. Rene did not generally look in this window. She did not generally go looking at clothes in shop windows at all. But it was Shirley's that stood opposite the end of Formby Road, where Rene waited at lunchtimes, torturing herself with the fear she would see the mirror image of her husband and his assistant. It was there she saw the coat, and she wanted it. Though there was no way she could afford it. Ted gave her enough money for the housekeeping, but the portion of this that was left after shopping for food and cleaning products had to keep the whole family in essential clothes. Luxuries were something Rene did not even allow herself to think about. Until she saw the coat.

On the third occasion she stood in front of the window, she did not turn and go home after the street had emptied. She pushed open the door of the shop. A bell tinkled. The shop smelled of lavender furniture polish. Rene walked up to the counter. She felt, in that moment, on the edge of something momentous.

'May I be of assistance, madam?' A woman with cascading auburn curls had pulled back the velvet curtain behind the shop counter and flashed a pasted-on smile at Rene. She was statuesque and wore a tight black dress with a low neckline.

Rene gulped. 'The coat...' she started, gesturing towards the window.

'The red bouclé, madam?' The assistant touched her spectacles with her right hand and made a moue with her mouth. Her lipstick was the vivid shade which, in her tortured fantasies, Rene imagined Madge wearing.

Rene nodded in a determined way. She had no idea what bouclé meant, but there was only one coat in the window.

'A beautiful coat, is it not? I'm so sorry, but it is on a reservation. Perhaps another coat, madam? We have a wide range.' She shimmied towards a rail of coats, all of which were dark-coloured.

Rene felt a wave of relief wash over her. 'No, no, thank you,' she said. 'I wanted a red coat.'

'Madam, there is—'

'No, thank you. It was just that one.' And she fled before the assistant had time to seduce her with another offer. Outside she stood for a moment or two leaning on the wall next to the shop, shocked at what might have happened if she had actually bought the coat. When she got home she made one of her special chocolate cakes for tea, but ate none of it herself. A sort of penance.

Rene stopped going to look in the window of Shirley's, afraid that the terrifying assistant would see her and lure her in with the promise of another red coat.

She did not encounter Madge again that year. Her night-time imaginings subsided, but she continued to punish herself – be it for her attempted stalking of Madge or the madness of even thinking of buying the red coat she could not have said – by not eating a single slice of any of the cakes she made.

'You're looking peaky,' Ted said to her one day. 'And you look after us all so well.' He put out his arm to draw her to him but, feeling tears coming from nowhere at the rare moment of attempted intimacy, she turned away.

And then, the next winter, there was the picture in the local paper. They'd done a feature about the factory, a double-page spread. Ted brought it home, proud as anything. And there he was, alongside his workmates, all standing outside the factory in two rows. Madge was at the end of the front row. The picture was in black and white, but there was no question: she was wearing the red bouclé coat with the fur collar.

There was a long dry spring after a dry winter and, come June, it started to warm up. Ted and Rene's daughters had exams and complained about being stuck indoors so much.

'It's bound to rain as soon as term's over,' said Peg.

But it didn't rain, and come July the two girls were outside all the time, home for meals and immediately off out again.

'Are they courting?' one of Rene's neighbours asked her.

'I certainly hope not,' she said. 'Dot's off to university in October, so long as she gets her grades. Studying sociology. First one in the family.'

It had been a bone of contention between Ted and Rene.

'I thought—'

But Rene had interrupted, 'I know, I know, you thought Dot would go into the family firm. Well, there's more to life than pots. And I don't suppose her sister will want to be stuck in that factory either.'

Ted hadn't wanted an argument. He did what he always did, went quiet. And Rene did what *she* always did, retreated into the kitchen.

Then things took another turn, as they do.

'I've got something to tell you, Mum,' Dot announced one day after tea, while she and her sister were still sitting at the table and Rene was folding her napkin. 'Hang on a minute, can you? And before you say anything, don't worry, there's no change of plan. I'm still going to Birmingham in the autumn. But—'

'But what?' Rene smoothed out her napkin and pressed her fingers down on it, looking across at her two daughters.

Dot hesitated, clenching her hands together in her lap.

'Come on, love,' said Rene, stretching out a hand.

There was a ring at the doorbell and Dot shot up to answer it. There was whispering in the hallway and then Dot came back into the dining room, a long-limbed young man trailing behind her. They stood there filling the doorway, him a full head taller than her. Rene pushed her chair back so she could get a proper look at the pair of them. Peg giggled and Rene snapped her head round to shush her. Dot lifted her chin in a defiant way. Then she pulled the lad to her side.

'This is Robert. He's got a place at Birmingham too he's reading geology and we're getting married.' The words came out in a rush, filling the room.

The boy – for what more was he than a boy?

Rene said to Ted afterwards – had the beginnings of a beard. He nodded and looked embarrassed, pressing his lips together and saying nothing.

Rene didn't know what to say either, her in her pinny and caught off guard with the dirty dishes from tea not yet cleared. All she could think of was that she didn't know what geology was any more than she knew anything about sociology, but she didn't think that either of them sounded as if they prepared you for a job of work.

Afterwards, when the lad had left, after some more whispering in the hall and a silence before the front door clicked shut, Rene found the words to say to Dot about how they were too young – and how on earth were they going to support themselves? – and they would regret it; and Dot said she was eighteen now and no one could stop her and she didn't care if her parents didn't come to the wedding because she loved Robert and–

'And what?' said her mother, who had noticed that her daughter's cheeks had filled out and her complexion was even more rosy than before, and felt the colour draining from her own cheeks as she realised.

'Well, so be it,' said Rene, because she knew now it was always best to be practical. 'Then you'd best get married as quickly as possible, and we'll say nothing to your father.'

The wedding happened in August. Dot made her own wedding dress, long, flowing and flowery, with balloon sleeves. Robert had grown quite a beard by then and wore a grey flared three-piece suit that was too big for him, with the university tie he'd bought in anticipation. Dot had a tan suede bell-bottomed trouser suit with a belted waist for her going away outfit. Not that she and Robert could afford to go away anywhere, what with the expenses they had to look forward to. And by the time Dot could get into that trouser suit again it had gone out of fashion.

They had colour photos of the day, though the grass wasn't green because of the drought. Rene remembered the heat, afterwards. It had made the asparagus rolls dry out and the sandwiches curl. Peg had made the cake and it was a shocker – every kind of colour swirled together in the sponge. Everyone said it tasted delicious though.

Of course they couldn't go to university, either of them. Robert got an apprenticeship as a plasterer and they both lived with Ted and Rene for the first year of their marriage. Cecily was born just before Christmas and immediately charmed her way into everyone's hearts.

# THE EIGHTIES

It was a commission, from someone in Italy. Apparently they'd picked up an old issue of *Vogue*, seen his work there. Wanted something "cutting edge". Ted got out his sketch book and created a brand-new design for a tall, sculptural vase, to be painted in bright colours.

'It's what we need, Madge, everyone needs a bit of a jolt from time to time. Avoids us getting in a rut,' he said to her, as they sat over their morning coffee. He always stopped for it, they couldn't risk spilling coffee on the workbench, and workers taking breaks was a catechism with him, part of his socialist principles. Everyone in the factory had a coffee break, and they sat together in the canteen with no separation between the bosses and the men and women on the production line. It made for a happy team, and a happy team was a produc-

tive team. That was the motto on their factory ban-
ner, the one they took out on the marches then,
and later too.

The new vase was more startling than anything
Ted had ever made before. After everyone in the
factory had gathered round and admired it, Madge
packaged it up and took it to the post office, and
off it went to Milan. They'd had a map out in the
canteen, everyone looking to see where it was, and
someone had a picture book. There was a photograph of a cathedral, white and shining, like a
fantastical wedding cake.

'To think that our work is going there!' said Ted.

And a few weeks later there came an envelope
with many stamps, postmarked Milano. Inside was
a letter in Italian and a photograph of the vase being
held by a boy who looked seven or eight years old.

*Qui è nostro figlio, Vincenzo*, said the letter.

'Here is our son.' The production line supervisor translated; he was keen on learning languages.
'I think Vincenzo is the Italian form of Vince,' he
said.

*Mille grazie.*

'A thousand thank yous.'

Ted told Rene about it, of course, but she
seemed particularly distracted that night, missing
the girls, who were off learning to lead separate
lives, Dot with her little girl and Peg away at col-

lege. He lifted his chin and tried to smile, but each time this happened he found it harder.

There were a lot of parties in 1984. But not everyone felt like celebrating. Just down the hill from Nelson Street where Ted and Rene lived, the striking miners gathered to march into town every Saturday. Rene watched from their bedroom window.

'Shocking,' she said.

'It is, love. Blooming awful. Just wretched what that woman has done to our country.' Ted came up behind her and put his arm around his wife's shoulders. Rene leant back against her husband and lifted her right hand to touch his fingers; since his heart attack things had softened between them. He had reduced his hours at the factory and they sat together more often in the evenings, her knitting and him reading. And they did talk, if not about everything. It was, in this second chance in their marriage, early days.

Come that May they had been married thirty years and their girls insisted there should be a party.

'You don't need to do anything, Mum,' Dot said when Rene protested that it was such a lot of work. 'Peg loves baking, you know she does. All you and Dad have to do is turn up.'

Rene did smile when she walked into the church hall. She smiled at all the friends and neighbours smiling at her, and she smiled at her lovely girls and her little granddaughter Cecily, and then she turned and smiled at Ted. It was as if the years had rolled away and it was the spring day when they had married. Except there was no lilac. The girls knew she hated it and they'd got white tulips and a flat pink flower Rene had never seen before.

'It's called a gerbera. From South Africa. Bringing us sunshine,' said Peg.

Rene thought it was a bit brash, and she liked English sunshine, but she didn't say that to her daughter. It was not a day for arguments.

After they'd all helped themselves to the buffet and the teapot had been round at least three times, there was a call to order from a man Rene did not recognise.

'Foreman, from the works,' Ted whispered in her ear. 'Sorry, love, there'll be a speech.'

The foreman, whose name was Shy, had a booming voice and his words fairly bounced off the walls of the hall, making the bunting quiver and shake.

'Comrades, ladies and gentlemen,' he started.

Ted stood. 'Mr Shy,' he said, 'before you say any more. We're all friends here today. So let's not be having any division between those we call comrades and those we call gentlemen.'

'And the women are comrades too,' called someone at the back, no one could quite see who.

There was a great muttering of assent, and Ted sat down and Mr Shy stood up again and got on with his speech with a good deal of jolly bluster; and when he finally sat down, puffing from the effort, Ted and Rene were called forward and Madge appeared from nowhere with a big box.

'It's from everyone for both of you, Mr and Mrs Marshall,' she said in a rush, her cheeks and neck reddening as they always did when eyes were on her. 'Mr Shy had it made, but it's from all of us.'

And she handed it over to Rene, whose smile had become rather fixed when she saw it was Madge making the presentation.

'Thank you,' she said.

'Thank you, my dear,' said Ted. 'Thank you everyone,' he said, turning to the room.

The friends and neighbours in the hall wanted to see the vase, they'd been told it was special, but Rene said they'd open it at home.

'Come on then, love, let's have a look-see now what they've given us,' said Ted as soon as they were home and had their coats off and the kettle on. The girls were still back at the hall, clearing up.

Rene pulled the vase out of the box. The design

was of lilac, purple lilac. She looked at it and her mouth moved a little, but she didn't speak. Ted looked at it and looked at his wife. He went to put his arm round her shoulders but she turned and went into the kitchen, clicking the door shut behind her. Ted sat down, put his elbows on the table and rubbed his right hand over his jaw, feeling the stubble that was always there by evening. After a while he put the vase back in the box and put the box in the cupboard of the sideboard. And then he went to the kitchen door. He listened. There was no sound. He called out to Rene, quite softly, that he was going up to bed, and he walked upstairs, holding on to the bannister rail, stopping halfway and putting his hand to his chest.

Two days after the anniversary party, it came on the one o'clock news that Eric Morecambe had died. It was a Sunday and Rene had just put lunch on the table. The Marshalls always had roast on a Sunday and it stuck in their minds afterwards that Rene had cooked a nice piece of brisket that day, which was always a tasty cut. Except that day neither of them seemed to have much of an appetite. They thought it must have been that sad news, on top of all the other bad news at that time, what with the miners' strike going on and on. And then Ted said:

'He wasn't all marvellous, you know. He supported Thatcher.'

'I don't care. I just loved Eric and Ernie, they made me laugh and we all need to laugh. You laughed at him too, Ted.'

'I did, I admit it. But you can't ignore a man's politics.'

The BBC put on a repeat of one of their Morecambe and Wise shows to commemorate Eric. The one when André Previn came on and Eric called him Mr Preview. Ted did laugh at that.

'What was his real name again?' Rene asked Ted. 'I know it wasn't Morecambe, though he was born here.' Ted said he couldn't remember. He was reading his paper, not really watching the rest of the programme.

'They ought to put up a statue to him,' said Rene.

'Maybe one day they will,' said Ted.

Rene picked up her knitting to get on with while they were watching Eric and Ernie. It was the pullover she'd started when Ted had his heart attack, the winter before. She'd put it aside and now she'd got a determination in her to get it finished. It was about proving something, something she couldn't put into words. But she knew she could put it into her knitting, could make it a lovely thing. She knitted it in red, knowing how much he liked that colour, though she'd gone off it herself.

'It's a good socialist colour, Rene,' he said. 'And you've made a good job of it.'

It was a way of showing she loved him. She wished she could say it, wished they could say it to one another, like they did in the early days. She didn't know what had happened to the words, why they wouldn't come out. But he did like that pullover, and he wore it for years. It lasted, like their marriage did, and when after a long time it got a hole in one of the elbows, the one he leant on at work, Rene darned it. She'd kept a bit of the wool back, with that in mind. And it held together. It held *them* together.

Our parents brought us up well. Dot and I were able to do what we wanted. After the war women were frightened of being left on the shelf. Mum's never said as much to me in as many words, but I know that in her day young women went to dances looking for a husband. I love my dad, and I know Mum loves him too, but I know as well that things haven't always been easy for them.

'Marriage is an up and down of a road,' Mum said to me once. 'I'd advise you not to go there.'

It was a shock, her saying that out of the blue. I was at college, home for the summer, feeling betwixt and between. I remember her sitting there, in the dim light of the dining room one evening, sitting upright and looking at me with a solemn face and her mouth turning down on one side. We'd just come back from a family holiday, in a caravan it was, down the coast. It was before Dad had his heart attack, I know that much. I don't remember much about the holiday. Just Dot's little girl making sandcastles on the beach and sand flying everywhere because she hadn't really got the hang of how to use the spade and me getting cross with her because I was trying to read, and Dot saying:

'Give over, Peg, she's not doing it on purpose. Anyway, you used to like making sandcastles with Dad when we were kids.'

My sister got married young. That was her choice, but I never wanted that road for myself, especially after what happened to her, left on her own with little Cecily. Don't get me wrong, she's a lovely child, but being an auntie's enough for me. I don't want kids of my own, can't be doing with cleaning up their mess any more than Dot's Robert could, though he had a responsibility, and what he did was wrong in my book. Me, I'm a free agent and I intend to stay that way; I don't need a man in my life.

I'm not saying nothing's ever happened. I have been in love. Well, I thought I was. It was at the first school I taught in. He was the head of department. Wore tweed jackets with suede patches on the elbows and smoked a pipe. I shiver thinking about it now, the tickle of the tweed on my cheek and the sweet smell of the tobacco. Because he told me then that he was married but that it was all over between them.

'You still live together, though?' I said.

'Yes, but like brother and sister.'

I didn't like the way he laughed when he said that. So casually. I said I wanted no more of it. He wheedled and I did see him again, but when he kissed me it wasn't the same. I got a new job the next term. I saw him quite recently, with a woman, arm in arm.

'Do you know that couple?' I asked the friend I was with. She confirmed what I suspected. That it was his wife.

I still don't know whether Mum and Dad had words, on that holiday. But I've wondered, off and on, about Madge, the girl who helps him at the factory. About whether there was anything.

Vincenzo Livio tells his mama he wants something special for his tenth birthday party. He's mad about football – already a member of his school team and dreaming of when he'll become a professional and play for Inter Milan – but he pulls a face when his mother suggests a cake decorated like a football.

'*Non sufficientemente speciale,*' he whinges, and flounces off to find a picture of the sort of cake he would like her to make.

'Ah, piñata cake!' exclaims his mama when he shows her the picture in a magazine. She's seen them in shop windows in the glass-domed gallerias – garishly-decorated sponge cakes cut open to show sweets hidden inside.

'*Farlo come un calcio, Mama,*' says the boy. He wants a cake like that in the shape of a football.

She loves her boy's enthusiasm and exuberance and she knows he will only be ten and carefree once. Soon will come the temptations of girls, and worse, and before she knows he'll be far away and she'll be crying. That night, when Vincenzo has gone to bed, she sits down with a piece of paper and a pencil and works out an idea to give him a birthday surprise that he will love.

Vincenzo's birthday is in March, and the white lilac trees in the square are in full bloom. His mama opens the windows of the flat to let in the scent drifting up on the spring breeze. She sends the boy and his little sister Sofia out into the square to play after lunch while she gets everything ready for the party: the balloons blown up, the table laid and, in pride of place, the traditional sweet-filled cardboard piñata – which is the shape and size of a large football and painted in the blues and yellows of the city's team – hanging from a hook in the ceiling.

At four o'clock she looks out of the window. Her children have been joined in the square by Vincenzo's friends and now they are all heading back for the party. Soon she hears the clomping of their footsteps on the stairs and then they're tumbling in.

'Hello, *buon* afternoon,' says a small boy she knows to be English, recently moved to Milano with his English mum and new Italian stepdad. Vincenzo's mama has met the boy's mum at the school gate. '*Buon pomeriggio*, Henry,' she smiles at him. 'And you must roll the "r"'.

'*Si, si,*' says the boy. 'Rrrrrrrr,' he says, with a toothy grin.

There are seven boys, and Sofia. Vincenzo at the head of the table.

'*Sorpressa!*' And there at the door is Vincenzo's papa, home early from work as a surprise for his son on his birthday, and the boy is hugging his legs and everyone is cheering as his father hands Vincenzo a big stick and encourages him to start whacking the hanging football. The piñata is strong; after five minutes Vincenzo is out of breath and the football cracked but still intact. The room is full of children jumping and screaming. Vincenzo lifts the stick, swings it behind his head and, with an almighty effort, brings it forward onto the cardboard ball, which bursts like a balloon, scattering cellophane-wrapped sweets and paper confetti around the room in a coloured snowstorm.

But there is something else falling. The children take no notice as they scramble for the sweets, but Vincenzo's backward swing of the stick has caught a vase that sits on top of a bookcase. His mother and father look at one another in horror as their beautiful English vase shatters on the parquet. Around them the party continues as before, for the carelessness of children in groups extends to feelings as well as possessions.

It is only later that Vincenzo cries, when all his friends have gone and his sister is already tucked up in bed. His mother tries to comfort him, says it doesn't matter, that she and his papa are not cross with him, they can get another vase, but he feels churned up inside, though he can't put into words what his feelings are.

Next day the boy tells his mama he doesn't want to play football anymore; he would rather take up dancing. His mother does not argue. She has no idea where this new enthusiasm has come from, but she isn't worried; she doesn't expect it to last long. It does last though, through the next birthday and the one after. It turns out that Vincenzo has a talent for ballet, and he begins to enter competitions and win prizes. He wins money, and he squirrels it away.

Vincenzo changes schools at the age of thirteen and his English friend Henry goes with him. He too is a dancer. Henry's Italian has improved fast, and he is teaching Vincenzo English. Neither of them seems to take any interest in girls, and their mothers, when they meet in the local supermarket, bring up the inevitable question.

'Yes, I think so,' replies the one.

'*Certo che si*,' says the other.

The women share little language but they both understand that their boys are more than just friends; it is not an issue for either of them, although they agree it will be best, for now at least, to say nothing to the boys' fathers.

Cecily wasn't yet thirteen when she told her grandmother she was a feminist and said she was never going to get married, it just led to problems.

'Look at my parents,' she said. 'Dad going off because he couldn't hack changing nappies!'

Rene didn't know all the ins and outs of why Robert had left Dot, but she thought it was probably true that he'd found having a baby around a good deal more complicated than the making of the baby in the first place.

'At least your dad keeps in touch,' she said.

'But Mum has to work. In a shop, for goodness' sake. It's not what she wanted. Or what I want.'

'Which is?'

'I'm going to be a writer. I've started, Gran.'

Rene didn't ask to see what Cecily was writing. Nor did she argue. The girl was bright. She'd be independent, have a career. Quite what it would be they'd see, all in good time.

# THE NINETIES

Cecily was a clever girl, always top of her class at school, destined for university, just as her mum had been. But Dot had sacrificed a good career for her daughter and Rene had been so disappointed, much as she loved Cecily. Her granddaughter wouldn't be so stupid, Rene was sure. Over the past few years they'd had lots of conversations about what she'd always thought was called women's lib, but Cecily said was much more complicated than That 1960s Stuff.

They went out for tea to celebrate Cecily's seventeenth birthday, the three of them. Dot said it was to be a mystery trip and it was still a mystery to Rene afterwards; she couldn't have said where they fetched up, so much did the country roads twist and turn around and back on themselves. But wherever it was it was lovely, an old ivy-covered hotel and, inside, a great log fire. The place decorated for Christmas, so tastefully, they all said.

'How clever of you to find this place, Mum,' said Cecily.

Sandwiches, scones and cakes arrived on a tiered stand and a soppy-looking golden retriever sat at their feet, waiting patiently for titbits.

When a few crumbs were all that was left and the dog was stretched out asleep in front of the fire, Rene asked Cecily about her plans.

'I've been looking forward to hearing,' she said. 'Which universities have you applied to? And have you settled on studying English? If you're going to a be a writer you're going to need—'

She stopped when she saw the strained expressions on the other women's faces. 'Oh no, you're not—'

Cecily brightened. 'No, no, Gran, I'm not getting married like Mum did, don't worry. And no, I'm not pregnant either.' She laughed and Dot gave a wry smile. 'Yes, I will be writing – I'm doing that already – but I'm not going to make my living that way. I'm going to travel for a few months next summer and when I'm eighteen I'm going to join Grandad in the firm.' She sat back and looked at Rene, clearly expecting her approval.

Rene didn't know what to say; her emotions were tumbling inside her. Dot patted her mother's hand and asked for more tea. The three of them sat sipping in silence.

Then Rene sat up very straight, put her hands together and bit her lip. 'Good,' she said. 'This much I'm glad about: it's a family firm and it's going to stay that way. But I hope you—' The weight of what she was about to say was pulling her face down, 'I hope you won't be content with second place.'

'Of course not, Gran. You know me. But I'll do my apprenticeship like everyone else. I'm not expecting preferential treatment; I know I have to learn.'

Dot frowned at her mother, but Rene had lowered her head and was lost in her thoughts and fears. The happy mood of the afternoon had been broken and their conversation became an inconsequential drift and dribble about Christmas presents. When they left the hotel the sun was setting over the distant hills, but not one of them could summon the energy to remark on its brilliance and beauty.

'Did you have a good time with Dot and Cecie?' asked Ted when he got home from work.

Rene didn't answer, just gestured to him to sit down for his meal before firing at him, 'Did you know Cecie was going to join the firm?'

Ted hesitated. 'Yes, but—'

'But what?'

'I knew you were hoping she'd go to university first, and I didn't want to upset you, so—'

'Well, you have. You have upset me.' Rene pushed back her chair and got up from the table, her face closed.

'I'm sorry, love,' he said. 'You know I never mean to—'

But Rene was out of the door before he could finish his sentence. Ted put his elbows on the table and his hands to his face. And, not for the first time, he wept.

Vincenzo's mama, like all Italian mamas, cries when her boy leaves home. He is seventeen, but still her *bambino*. But he must do what he must do, he and his friend Henry have done so well to get into ballet school in Rome, she is so pleased, they are both lovely boys. She says these things to her neighbours, but still she cries.

In Rome the boys find a fourth-floor garret to rent. There is a concierge with startlingly black eyebrows who shushes them when they talk loudly on the stairs, and a stooped elderly woman on the floor below who brings them food and speaks in a Roman dialect Henry finds difficult to understand.

'Away from your mamas,' she's saying; Vincenzo translates for his friend. 'You need feeding up.'

They tell her it won't do for dancers to get fat, and they crumble her special cakes for the birds in the park in their lunch breaks, but she will not be dissuaded. Vincenzo, who has always had a sweet tooth, finds that he is loving *la signora*'s food more than he is enjoying the rigours of ballet training. One night he and Henry come home late and Vincenzo goes straight to the fridge.

'You're not going to eat?!' says Henry.

'Is that an order?' says Vincenzo. He laughs, but his friend puts out his hands and seizes him at the elbows, his face sombre.

'Have you not seen the new boys?'

'Meaning?' Vincenzo laughs again. 'Oh, so there's one you are fancying more than me, he has a tight little—' He searches for the word in English and doesn't find it, '*culo.*'

Their argument does not change anything; it was changing anyway. Within weeks Henry has moved out of the apartment. Vincenzo eats more and more of *la signora*'s pastries and pastas. He knows where it is all leading. He starts cutting classes and takes on more hours at the bar where he works at weekends; by the end of May he is there full-time.

'*Ciao*,' say the boys from the ballet school when they come in for their morning coffee. But their friendliness is superficial; they stop including him in their chatter, for he is no longer one of them. And Henry has his morning coffee elsewhere.

Vincenzo tries out different things and different people. He is neither happy nor unhappy; life is, he tells anyone who enquires, amusing. He hardly notices time passing. He is still of an age when he takes everything and everyone for granted. Until his sister Sofia calls and berates him for being so selfish and never calling his mama. He tells her to leave him alone, promises to telephone more often, and fails to do so. And then, a year on – or is it two? – his papa dies. Amongst the black coats at the funeral he sees Henry. Still-beautiful Henry. They meet the next day for a coffee. After that, back in Rome, they meet again, but as friends now, not lovers.

'Is there other person?' Vincenzo asks, wistfully.

'Another person, you should know by now that's what we say in English,' says Henry, laughing when he sees Vincenzo's crestfallen face. It's a gentle laugh though, and kind. 'No, no, there's no one else. But I'm going to England. Don't look sad, I promise I'll write. I'll do it partly in Italian, and you'll write to me and keep up your English, won't you?'

Henry keeps his promise. Vincenzo looks forward to the letters, full of gossip about the dance world. That is the bit he misses, not the hard work. He admires his old friend for having the discipline he never had, is proud of him, tells his colleagues in the bar where he works about the shows that his English friend dances in. The years go by, and Vincenzo pushes from his mind the thoughts that come sometimes about how he could have had another life, one that might have been more fulfilling. If only.

Three more swirls of blue, a little yellow flourish below, and the EM of his signature. The last ever Edward Marshall vase, completed. Ted sat back, dazed at the thought that this was to be his last work for the firm. Fifty years gone in a turn of the wheel.

Spontaneous applause broke out behind him. Ted rose on his creaky knees, turned slowly and gave a little bow. He loved these people. How many could say that of their work comrades? How many even thought of them as comrades? But for Ted it was the truth. Together they were one of the last of their kind, a family firm: S & L Marshall, Ceramicists, his grandfather and aunt, then him.

His daughters had their own interests, but his granddaughter Cecily was there. She would carry on the name. She was nearly twenty-five and had been working in the factory for several years already, serving her apprenticeship as everyone had to do. Ted had heard the odd mutter amongst the workers about Cecily being "just a slip of a girl", but he was having none of that. He reminded them about his Aunt Lavinia.

'This factory was set on its feet by a woman, and I'm proud that we'll have a woman at the helm again,' he said at the little do they'd put on for him. 'You're all good folk, and I know you'll support her.'

'I'm proud of you too, Grandad,' Cecily said in her speech over the sandwiches and the fancy cakes. And Madge, dear old Madge – though goodness, how could he say that? She must be twenty years younger than him – was there, hopping from foot to foot and holding out a ridiculously big box.

'Don't drop it, Madge!' the men cried out as one, though they knew she never would. Ted pulled the ribbon and the shiny paper fell away. He lifted the lid, peeked inside, and his eyes widened. There, nestling in tissue paper, was a wonder of ceramic construction, Blackpool Tower in the form of a teapot.

'Madge designed it,' cried Cecily. 'Isn't she clever?'

'And don't you drop it either, Mr Marshall!' someone at the back shouted out as Ted thrust it aloft as if he were the first Englishman to win the Men's Singles Trophy at Wimbledon for over fifty years.

People said afterwards that they had never seen Ted Marshall smile so widely or for so long. And what a shame that Rene had not been there for his send-off, to see how happy he was, there in his factory with all his comrades around him. He said, with a little twitch of his mouth, that Rene had not been feeling so good that morning. They didn't ask, not Madge or any of the others. They had too much respect for their boss to pry into the sorrows of his marriage.

When all the fancy cakes had been eaten, one of the men magicked a bottle of whisky and a tray of small glasses from under a table.

'Time to drink a toast in something stronger than tea, lad,' said the man, whose name was Small, although he was a broad, tall fellow.

A doubtful 'Oh!' was all that Ted could muster in reply. But Rene and her disapproval were not there, so there was nothing to stop him.

'It's not as if you retire every day,' said Madge, downing a second glass, thrilled by the warm flush the first had given her.

Ted looked at Madge, cheery, marvellous Madge, and wondered how he was going to manage without her.

'You'll come over and see us, won't you?' he said. 'Rene will be pleased if you do.'

Madge just nodded. They both knew Rene would not be pleased if she did. It was a crying shame.

'You've been a marvel,' Ted said to Madge as he picked up his coat. What he wanted to say was that he loved her, that he'd loved her for years and she should get her coat too and they'd leave together and go... anywhere, anywhere other than these dull streets. Somewhere they could be free, walk together arm in arm every day and live in a bunga- low by a warm sea and eat fried chicken and pizza pie and drink whisky every evening if they wanted...

Ted could no more have said these things than he could have flown through the air like one of the gulls of Morecambe Bay, though once he had dreamt he had done so, and when he woke the next morning he had thought for the briefest of sweet moments that it was Madge beside him in the bed.

He told himself, as he walked home carrying the enormous box that contained the teapot in the shape of Blackpool Tower, that no one could deprive him of his dreams. Before he let himself into the house he stowed the box and its contents in the garage. He did not want to hear Rene's sar- castic comments. He was not going to give her that pleasure. He would arrange – he would think of a way – for the teapot to be taken to a charity shop somewhere far away, somewhere no one from the factory would ever see it. When Rene asked about his present he would say he had been given tokens. He knew she wouldn't ask what they were for.

I had my thoughts about leaving. Show me a married woman who hasn't. But thinking and doing are two different things and I was brought up to be loyal. Which I was, right till the end.

The night I met Ted at the Palais I had a new frock. I'd sewn it myself and it had three different materials in it: organza underneath, taffeta for the skirt, and satin for the trimmings. The organza was from an old petticoat of my mother's, but the rest I'd saved up for and bought in Mrs Harding's Haberdashery, buttons and a zip fastener too. The frock was peach-coloured. When I put it on for the first time and twirled in front of my parents, Father said it made me look peachy and I don't know what shade of pink my face turned!

I couldn't afford new shoes but, young and naïve as I was, I knew one thing – boys' eyes were not going to be on my feet. I met my friend Phyllis on the corner as arranged and we walked together into town. I can feel the excitement now, writing about it. It was summer and warm. We didn't need coats, but I took a cardie, just in case. That wasn't new either, but I wasn't going to be wearing it while I was dancing.

I spotted Ted as soon as I arrived. He was hanging back from the other lads, listening to the band.

I liked that about him. I liked the shy ones. A great clumsy girl – I think she might have been called Susie or Judy, I didn't know her – got hold of him in a Ladies' Excuse Me. I saved him from her. It wasn't meant to be for life, only that dance. But one thing led to another, like it does.

They say that your wedding day is the happiest day of your life. Maybe for some people. My bouquet was a mess. I don't know who chose lilac. I don't even like the colour, never mind that cloying smell. I would have preferred the flowers to be peach-coloured, like that frock. I did cut a length from its satin sash and tie it on my leg as a kind of garter, my Something Old. I thought it might be, you know, helpful on our wedding night, but Ted was embarrassed. He undressed in the dark. Always did, all our married life.

I suppose if we'd talked more. But what with the cooking, the cleaning, the washing and then the two children, so four of us to keep in clean outer and underwear, how could there have been time for talking?

I've always done my best and I expect Ted thought he had too. We did have our moments. But when I look at our wedding photos, the standing-side-by-side photos, I just feel sad. Because I could have married someone else, he wasn't the only fish in the sea. I told Ted that, more than once, and it made him cry. I suppose it must have been hard to hear, but there were plenty of things that made *me* want to cry too.

A marriage is a journey with unexpected turnings. You're rubbing along all right and one day you get a letter. It was a poison pen letter, bits chopped out of newspapers, just like in a story. There was a woman at the factory it said. That she and Ted had been, you know. I burned it. I've never told anyone. And then that phone call. I didn't believe it. Not that Madge. Impossible. But it sowed a seed in my heart and the plant that grew from that seed bore a bitter fruit. I had the taste of it in my mouth for years. I'm afraid Ted will still keep in touch with her even though he's retired. But I'd rather not know.

# THE NEW MILLENNIUM

It was easy for people to make judgements about Madge Turner. To call her dumpy. To call her dowdy. And then there were the sly comments behind her back. Gossip about her and Ted. Madge wasn't a stupid woman; she knew what people said. But she didn't let any of it touch her. She loved her work, from the earliest days. She'd gone into the factory straight from school, not knowing what to do. She wasn't brainy, but she was good with her hands, nifty with a needle and a paintbrush.

'It'll be a nice little job until you find out what you really want to do with your life, or meet your husband,' her mother said.

Mrs Marshall senior was tall, slender and smartly dressed. She was smart about people too – she saw the potential in Madge straight away, set her to work with Ted.

'You'll get on well,' his Aunt Lavinia said to Ted. 'She'll be a steady worker.'

And they did and she was, from the first to the last. Madge didn't want a husband. She knew that Ted's wife had given up work when they'd married, as her own mother had. The first time she'd met Mrs Marshall junior she could feel the tension and unhappiness in her. She felt sorry for her, though she knew Ted was devoted to his wife and his children.

'I've got a wonderful family. And I'm so lucky to have you alongside me at work, Madge,' he said. 'You've been the making of me.'

It made her blush. She was in love with him from the day they met, though she never told a soul. It didn't make her unhappy, that was the magic. It was something she held inside herself, like a warm hug. She would have liked his arms around her, of course she would, to have had him next to her on her walks along the seafront, to sit side by side on her little sofa after supper in the evenings. But she didn't, and knew she never would, and that was that. Madge was a dreamer, but she was also realistic. She wasn't lonely at weekends, because she had Monday mornings to look forward to.

Madge sewed her own clothes, neat skirts and blouses that she wore under her work overalls. She had no need of anything fancy. But she did buy a coat. She saw it in the window of Shirley's, the shop she'd walked past every day for five years on her way to and from work and had never before dared enter. But this coat called to her, a beacon in the dark. It was red, and it had a fur collar. Some boldness latent in her made her walk straight in the door and up to the forbidding woman who stood behind the counter.

'I'd like to try on the coat in the window, please.'

'Of course, madam.' If the assistant had an opinion about her unlikely customer, she did not betray it. She told Madge the coat suited her and took £5 to reserve it.

Madge saw the coat as an investment; it would last her. And it did, through all the winters till her retirement and beyond. It was a good warm coat, kept out the cold of the wind that blew off the waters of the bay in winter. Though the fur of the collar tickled more than it comforted. That, she supposed, was the price she had to pay for imagining herself to be better than she was.

After Ted retired he kept in touch, but it wasn't the same. Madge had nothing to look forward to on Mondays any more. She got a dog. A Jack Russell. She called him Teddy. Walked him on the prom. Past the statue of Eric Morecambe. Madge liked the statue, him dancing on one leg. Though of course he didn't have his partner either. That made her sad. She avoided talking to anyone she saw near the statue, just kept her head down and carried on walking.

When they were clearing out the old factory – changed times meant they had to move to smaller premises – someone found a diary stuck in the back of a desk drawer. One of the apprentices took it to the new boss.

'I don't know whether you want to take a look at this, Mrs Marshall.'

Cecily used her grandfather's name; the firm had always been S & L Marshall and she had no intention of changing that, however much else had to change for them to keep their place in the ceramics market.

Cecily thanked the lad. When he'd gone, she felt the weight of the book in her hands and ran her fingers over the smooth, faded red leather of its cover. Five Year Diary, it said in embossed, scuffed gold letters. She opened it. The pages were covered in small, neat handwriting. Flicking back, she saw the name written on the flyleaf, frowned, then snapped the book shut and dropped it into her handbag as a shadow appeared behind the opaque glass of her office door.

'You've been with the firm for over ten years, haven't you?' she said to the man who had come to tell her that the removal men were ready to take her office furniture. 'Do you remember Marjorie Turner?'

The man pursed his lips and looked up to the left. 'Marjorie, Marjorie... No... Yes... Turner.... that was the name of your grandfather's assistant. Madge, she was always called. Very quiet. Terribly loyal. A stalwart, he always said. What about her, has she died or something?'

'No, no, nothing like that, I just saw the name on a letter...' Cecily's voice tailed off, then she recovered herself.

'OK now, desk first?' said the removal men, muscling into the room.

'Come on,' Cecily said to her secretary, who was hovering in the doorway looking anxious. 'Let's go and get a cup of tea. No point in getting sentimental about the old place.'

Cecily's husband was out that night, at a book group. She warmed up the casserole he'd left her and poured herself a large glass of Shiraz. The TV offered a choice between the usual soaps and worthy-sounding documentaries. Cecily channel-hopped, conscious all the time of the diary in her bag. She pulled it out and opened it at random.

*1969*

*March 6*

*Mr Marshall asked me to turn on the wireless. There was a tune called something like A Persian Market. It was so exotic and rousing. After that there was something quieter which almost made me cry. Mr M saw that. I felt a thrill go all the way through me. I excused myself before*

There was something scored out after that. Cecily flicked forward in the diary.

*1970*

*January 6*

*Back to the factory after the Christmas break. So happy to be back. A whole new decade ahead of us!!! Mr Marshall let slip that*

Something scored out again. There were a lot of similar entries. The very last one was

*1972*

*April 30*

*I read in the paper that there was a big band at the Winter Gardens. I told Mr Marshall. He looked at me and for a minute I thought*

The last two lines were scored out. Cecily closed the diary and poured herself another glass of Shiraz. There were things she had heard. Rumours, gossip about her grandparents and their marriage. She'd always discounted what people said as jealous tittle-tattle, always thought Ted and Rene were devoted to one another. Now she wondered. Madge had been, what? Ten years younger than Ted? No, more. In 1972 he'd been... she worked it out... thirty-eight. Madge only eighteen, for goodness sake. But the age gap meant nothing. People had affairs at all ages. And hopes and dreams and fantasies at all ages. So maybe Madge had been in love with Ted. What harm would that have done? But what if they'd actually had an affair? And what if, even supposing they hadn't, her grandmother Rene had thought they had?

Cecily sat thinking about all this until her husband got home, feeling sorry, in the end, for all three of them.

'You look pensive. Listen, pour me out the end of that bottle. I have to tell you about our book for next month.'

And he bounced down onto the settee, so enthusiastic, so lively, so real, pulling his wife to him. Cecily laughed.

'And what's so funny?' he said.

'Nothing... you... no, nothing, I can't explain.'

Nor could she. And the past was the past. Gone. And yet. That night, as she lay in bed, Cecily thought about Ted, and Rene, and Madge, and about love and hope and disappointment. Then she turned to her husband, snoring gently by her side, and hugged him tight. He woke with a start.

'Were you having a bad dream?' he said.

'No, no, just thinking. Promise me,' she said, suddenly fiercely passionate. 'Promise me you'll always talk to me.'

'Of course I will, silly,' he said. And she wrinkled her nose and he kissed it.

'I love you,' he said. 'Go to sleep now.'

'I love you too. Sleep tight.'

Next day Cecily was busy with all the upheaval of the removal at the factory. She didn't think about the diary again until she got home and saw it on her desk. Then she made a few phone calls and discovered that Madge was still living in Morecambe. When her husband got home from work she told him the whole story.

'I don't know what to do,' she said. 'Should I return the diary to her?'

There was rain veiling the bay and spitting in their faces when they got off the bus.

'We'd best get lunch straightaway,' said Ted. 'No point in getting soaked. I fancy fish, no chips, just fish. This place'll do, won't it, Mum?'

He tinkled open the door of a café with a peeling signboard before Rene could say otherwise. The place looked to her as if it hadn't changed since the fifties. There were lacy curtains, pictures of old Morecambe on the walls, and crusted ketchup bottles on the tightly crammed tables.

'This'll do us nicely,' Ted said.

Rene thought she would have preferred somewhere a bit classier, seeing as they were on a day out. But she didn't say so.

There were sardines on the menu. Deep-fried, with some kind of sauce. A fancy name Rene hadn't heard of. She thought about having them, though she knew she shouldn't eat deep-fried. And neither should Ted. She didn't say so, because she knew that if she did, he'd say to stop going on.

Rene decided on the liver and Ted um'd and ah'd for a long time, she really couldn't see why, after he'd said he wanted fish. Eventually he made a big fuss about calling the waitress over, said he hoped she wasn't too busy to take their order and they'd have the sardines and the liver and a pot of tea for two.

'Please,' Rene added, and he gave her a look. 'What?' she said.

'Nothing,' he said.

They were sitting at a table near the front window and Rene was looking out at the sea. There were little squealing noises as the rain spattered the window. Then the door clanked open and in came the noise of the rain louder and two men who shook themselves like dogs. One of them grimaced at Rene.

'Nice day for ducks,' he said.

'It is,' she said. 'Have you been to see the statue?'

'We have. Did you know it was bigger than life-size?'

Ted was pursing his mouth and giving Rene a look, so she bent down as if to pick something up from the floor. By the time she'd straightened up again the two men had gone to sit at the back of the café and, before Ted could start, the dinner came.

Rene thought the liver was quite nice. There was just one fish on Ted's plate, that and the sauce, which looked like salad cream with bits in it. The fish was flattened out, like someone had walloped it with the back of a spoon. Ted picked at it with his fork.

'I thought there'd be several fish,' he said.

Rene had thought that too, but she didn't say so, just got on with her liver. The couple at the back were giving their order. One of them sounded foreign to her. The rain was hitting the window harder as if it was turning to hail.

'Must be disappointing to come all this way and then have it rain,' she said.

Ted didn't look up from his fish. Rene went to pour out the tea.

'Wait, Mum, we'll have it after.'

Rene thought she would have liked hers with the liver, which was a bit dry. Ted carried on eating.

'This has got a good fish to crust ratio,' he said.

He seemed to have got over there being only one. Rene thought she would have liked to try it. She'd chosen liver, and that was what she'd got. Like it or lump it, Ted would have said.

'Don't know why you wanted liver,' he said. 'I couldn't eat anything that had originated inside a person.'

'It isn't from a person, it's pig's liver.'

'Yes, OK, but you know what I mean, Mum.'

Rene didn't say that he'd eaten liver plenty of times in the past and not complained.

When they'd finished eating, Ted asked Rene if she was never going to pour out the tea. It was a bit stewed by then, which was hardly surprising, but she knew he liked it that way. She liked her tea weak. The tea seemed to perk Ted up and he got suddenly chatty and came out with something Rene had never heard before. He said that Eric

Morecambe loved shellfish. What was more, he said, and she might not know this, Eric had written a best-selling book about fishing. Really? she said. She was glad he'd told her those things. Somehow, they helped to keep the magic alive.

The rain had eased off and Ted said they'd best go and see the statue. It was true, it did look bigger than life-size, Eric dancing on one leg with binoculars round his neck. It was up some steps, which Ted said probably made it look bigger, and there was some bloke sweeping the steps. He said it was the most photographed sight in the world, which Rene thought was unlikely, especially given there were just the three of them there, but perhaps he knew. He offered to take their picture with Eric and, to Rene's surprise, Ted let him.

'We could have another cuppa, Mum, if you like,' Ted said as they walked away along the prom. The sun was setting over the Fells. They stood for a moment, looking out across the water, thinking their own thoughts.

The café was all locked up and they couldn't see anywhere else, but what with that lovely view across the bay and the photo they'd have to show people, and Ted setting up whistling one of Eric and Ernie's old songs, Rene felt a bit of a warm glow in the bus going home, and she put her arm through his and he let her.

Henry doesn't write to Vincenzo so often now, and his communications, such as they are, are by email. Then comes this one.

'You are not going to believe this!' says Henry's message. 'I've got a job on *Strictly*. We are in Blackpool in October. You have to come.'

Henry phones the day after the email arrives, which is as well, because Vincenzo has no idea where Blackpool is.

'The Tower Ballroom in Blackpool! It's famous! And fabulous!' gushes his friend.

'But, Blackpool? Where is?'

Henry says it's in the north of England and Vincenzo is none the wiser.

But he says, 'OK, *benissimo*, and so *Strictly*, what is?'

'It's going to be amazing. They had this programme on the TV in England, way back. *Come Dancing*, it was called. Ballroom and Latin. All the pros were in it. This is an update, glitzy, and with celebs partnering the pros. I tell you, it's going to be a sensation.'

Vincenzo looks it up, this *Come Dancing* programme. He writes back to Henry.

'Is what you call fuddy-duddy, this old programme. I no think I come.'

'NO, NO, NO, you didn't listen, *amico* – it's an update. Look, preview's next week. You'll see. I'll send you a clip.'

And he does so, and Vincenzo grudgingly has to admit that it does look different from the swirling sedateness and bouffant hair-dos that were his idea of ballroom dancing, from the pictures he's seen in books. And he rather likes the glitter, and the costumes. Perhaps, he thinks, he will go.

Three months later Vincenzo flies to London and travels on to Blackpool by train.

'It's been too long,' says Henry when he meets his friend at the station. 'Ten years, would you believe?'

The Tower Ballroom is as stunning as Henry said it would be. As is the show.

'Is not bad, your partner,' says Vincenzo. 'You reckon you win?' He winks.

'OK, I know what you're getting at, but she knows how I am, and as for winning the competition, I doubt it. But I'm having the best time.'

The two of them have fun in the week that follows. Henry has rehearsals with his partner, a minor celebrity who's a presenter on TV in Manchester, so it suits him to stay up in Blackpool. While his partner is at work, he and his old friend have days out. They take a train north to Kendal, then a bus and walk up onto the Lakeland Fells, till they're high on the crags of Scout Scar and Henry points out Blackpool Tower, which looks like a toy on the horizon. They find a hollow out of the wind to sit and eat their sandwiches and lie back in the autumn sunshine. There's no one else up there. Contrails crisscross the sky, but the planes are too high to be heard. The only sounds are the twitterings of the birds. Vincenzo and Henry lie side by side, thinking their own thoughts.

On the way down they're still quiet, but when they get down onto the flat, walking towards the bus stop, Vincenzo puts his arm through his friend's and as they exchange smiles he thinks this must be what it's like to be one half of an old married couple. He's about to say that to Henry when they see the bus coming, and they run to catch it.

The next day they go to Morecambe. It's raining, so they take a quick look at the statue of Eric, get the chap who's sweeping the steps to take their photo and then go into a café on the front for lunch. It's quite old-fashioned, but Vincenzo likes that, and sitting there across the table from Henry it's almost like old times. Except of course times have changed and they both know that.

At the end of the week Vincenzo goes back to Italy, picks up again where he left off. But he's restless;

he goes travelling, goes to Asia and sees a lot of temples and spends too many nights in seedy hotels. Nothing satisfies him. He goes home to his mama in Milan. The city that used to seem so big now feels confining.

'What you want?' shouts his sister Sofia, over the noise being made by her *bambini*.

'*Non lo so*– I don't know,' he says. One thing he knows for sure is that there is no future for him in Milan. And goes back to Rome. But at the bar where he used to work there's a new manager, a new regime. The manager is clearly younger than Vincenzo – he looks him up and down and asks whether he has experience of roller skating. Looking round, Vincenzo sees he's not joking and turns on his heel. As he goes out of the bar a group of young people are passing. They have about them something he remembers from his early days in the city with Henry, something light and carefree that he has lost.

He goes into a bar and asks for a *caffè corretto* – coffee with alcohol. It is three o'clock, too early to be drinking, but who's to know, and he doesn't care. There's an English newspaper lying on a table and he picks it up and flicks through the pages. On page seven, there are pictures of a seaside town in England. There's a little photo of a statue of a man dancing on one leg. *The Famous Eric Morecambe*, it says. He recognises it, reads the article. It's about Morecambe, the place he went to with Henry on that rainy day, the place they ate fish in an old-fashioned café and had their picture taken alongside the statue. There was something about that place, even in the rain. Or maybe, he thinks, it was just nostalgia, being with Henry, having those days out, as if...

The reason for the article is that there's a hotel that's been renovated. Art deco, says the piece. It does look rather splendid in the photos, the clean white lines of the exterior and the sophisticated elegance of the interior. Oh, to have lived in the 1920s, thinks Vincenzo, in the Jazz Age, to have mixed with F Scott Fitzgerald and Hemingway in the South of France. He pulls himself up, cross at this useless reverie. He is living in the twenty-first century, and he needs a job. And then, suddenly, he knows exactly what he will do.

It is just three weeks later that Vincenzo Livio, dressed in his best suit and highly polished shoes, presents himself at the reception desk of the Midland Hotel, Morecambe.

'I am here to see the manager,' he says, in his best English accent. 'About his job.'

The receptionist smiles. She is polite; she knows what Vincenzo means.

'Sandra,' she calls to a waitress, 'please can you

show Mr Livio through?'

Sandra smiles too, and takes Vincenzo to the manager's office. Outside the big windows there are sea birds, wheeling, and the sun is glinting on the wide waters of Morecambe Bay. He smiles now, cautiously, hoping this will be the beginning of a new chapter, not just another job.

It is a quiet morning at the Midland Hotel. The duty manager has set fresh gerbera blooms in vases. One flower in each vase on each small table in the coffee lounge. They are flashes of colour, orange, yellow and pink, in the monochrome of the restored art deco interior, pictures of which adorn the pages of glossy magazines in London, Paris and New York. There are people who read these magazines and decide to come and visit Morecambe, to stay in this famous hotel, to see the seahorses on its façade designed and carved by Eric Gill, and to admire the views across the bay. But these people come in summer. They do not come in this season, this tail-end of autumn, not-quite-pre-Christmas, dark, damp season when the clouds lie low over the bay and the hills of the Lake District are visible only as a slight change in distant coloration, possibly more imagined than real.

The duty manager today is Vincenzo. He is finding Morecambe difficult in autumn. He did not find it much easier in summer. It was busier and brighter, but not gayer, not in the way he would have liked. He talks to his friends back in Italy on WhatsApp and they tell him he should go to Brighton, where the scene will be more to his taste. Too late. He has a contract with the Midland Hotel, where he attends to the needs of elderly people on coach outings. In between coach parties few people come through the doors of the hotel in this season, and Vincenzo likes to stand by the big picture windows and watch the gulls. He likes the way they are free, the way they are naughty. If he were a gull he too would swoop down and steal chips from the elderly. But he is a duty manager at the Midland Hotel and his job requires him to be polite to all his customers, however annoying. Sometimes there are weddings, but not at this time of year. Funerals are more common, and just today someone has called to book a funeral tea, the second for her family in three weeks. He tells her, quite genuinely, how sorry he is.

A woman has come in this morning with a small, yappy dog in a handbag. Dogs are not allowed in the Midland Hotel, even in handbags. Sandra, the coffee waitress, has told the woman this but she is still there, sitting at a table in the lounge. She has let the dog out of her handbag and it nearly trips Sandra up as she is carrying a full tray of hot coffees. She rings through to Vincenzo, who is on his own coffee break and is not pleased to be disturbed, as he has reached a racy passage in his novel.

'Why not you fix her?' he snaps at Sandra. His English is not of the standard which the top management of the Midland Hotel would prefer, but they have to take who they can get these days.

'She ain't taking no notice of me.' Sandra's English also has its deficiencies, but she has a winning smile. The visiting coachloads always like her. She likes them. She does not like the woman with the small, yappy dog. She thinks it is a miniature schnauzer, she tells Vincenzo, as if that will help him to deal with the woman.

The quick tap-tap of Vincenzo's shoes on the parquet floor makes the woman look up from the glossy magazine she is flicking through. She raises a quizzical eyebrow.

'I is a-sorry, madam,' he starts, but she is jabbing a purple-varnished fingernail at a photograph in the magazine. A photograph of this very lounge in the Midland Hotel, in which a number of people in beachwear are sitting at small tables. Beside one of the people is a dog. In the background of the picture, but without question a dog.

Vincenzo frowns. 'Madam, that is a photograph taken in our summer, when our lounge open itself onto the terrace. The dogs are permitted,' he says with a note of triumph, 'only on the terrace.'

The woman sniffs but does not move. When, eventually, she leaves, Vincenzo smells something unpleasant and discovers its source under the table. He asks Sandra to clear up the mess and removes the offending magazine.

The rest of the morning is uneventful. If anything, the clouds descend a little further. There is no one walking on the beach. The gulls seem listless, rising only for brief squawky forays before returning to their perches and fluffing up their feathers against the day.

At lunchtime Vincenzo, on an impulse, and feeling himself in debt to Sandra after the business with the dog, invites her to go out with him for a sandwich. She, secretly, finds Vincenzo rather attractive, but she knows there is no point in getting her hopes up in that direction. She is, nonetheless, pleased to be asked. They cross the road to a café where the sandwiches are twice the size and half the price of those at the Midland Hotel, even taking the staff discount into account. Vincenzo finds that Sandra is a good listener. Sandra feels useful. They both return to their duties after lunch with a lighter heart.

In the afternoon a coachload from Scotland turns up a day early. Sandra flashes her smile at the kitchen staff and they magic up high tea for forty people. The tourists eat their fill, heap praise on the Midland Hotel, and leave munificent tips for Sandra and Vincenzo.

At the end of the day Vincenzo walks Sandra to the bus stop. His bus goes in the opposite direction, but as he journeys back to his bedsit he realises that, for today at least, he is content.

# IN THE END

It was pneumonia that took them off in the end. Dad first, and Mum only three weeks later. I think she was literally heartbroken. They'd been together for over fifty years. My sister has a theory about Dad having a fancy woman at the factory, but I don't believe it for one moment; she always did have an over-active imagination, our Peg, and anyway, when I've asked her to elaborate, she won't. Fact is, Dad was devoted to Mum. He was devoted to the factory too, it's true, but our Cecily's running it now and he'd be chuffed to bits how well she's doing. I say he'd be chuffed – he was! Used to go in twice a year after he retired, just before the factory fortnight holiday and at Christmas, to see his old comrades as he called them. His assistant Madge worked on after she reached sixty, she was that devoted to the place, only retired herself two

95

or three years ago. I remember Dad went to the pub with her and the others after her leaving do. Mum tut-tutted about it, said he'd come home half-cut. By which she meant he'd had a couple of pints. Mum never touched alcohol apart from a ginger wine at Christmas, just to be sociable.

My sister and I cleared out the house. Peg found it upsetting being there in our old family home, empty and cold now, and wanted to get off as quickly as possible, so I took the old photographs away with me to sort through. In the wedding album Mum looks misty-eyed, though maybe that's the poor quality of the pictures. Lilac, she was carrying. Hardly what you'd choose for a bouquet these days. Our Cecie had those lovely gerberas. You have to wire them. They could have done that with the lilac, florists must have had wire even in 1954. Though perhaps they didn't use a florist. That's it. Grandma Marshall did the flowers, Dad's mum. I remember now, Mum said it put *her* mum's nose right out of joint, what with Grandma Marshall preparing the wedding breakfast as well. She got hold of all sorts of food they hadn't seen since before the war, if then, and it must have been amazing. I think Mum said she even had a pineapple – how exotic was that in the fifties?

Why do we talk about wedding breakfasts, but funeral teas? You always have to wait for ever before you get fed at a wedding, these days at least. Might as well be the next day's breakfast before you're done. For Mum's and Dad's funerals we went to the Midland Hotel for a bite. Mid-afternoon both times, so I don't know what you'd call that, tunch maybe.

I'd been to the Midland for coffee with a friend only the week before Dad died and they'd gerberas on the tables, just like in Cecie's wedding bouquet. Nice and bright. I don't know, to be honest, if Mum or Dad ever went there in real life, so to speak. They probably would have thought it a bit posh. Actually, it's lovely. The manager was Italian, and so polite. I couldn't fault him, nothing too much trouble. Same with the lovely waitress.

And another thing, why don't people take photographs at funerals, I wonder? Mum never was that keen on having her picture taken. There are more of Dad. Him with me riding on his shoulders when I was three or four. Him with Peg and me building sandcastles on a beach, not Morecambe, somewhere with cliffs. Terrible swimming trunks he was wearing. All baggy. There are no photos of them together except standing stiffly and unsmiling in group shots at other people's weddings. But what a smile on Dad's face at his retirement do! I don't think I've ever seen that photo before. They should have had it framed, but then Mum wasn't one for what she called "all that clutter". Just more stuff to dust, she would have said.

We're all different. Look at me and Peg. People say they'd never know we were sisters. I've no complaints. I had a happy childhood. There's just the odd thing. Once or twice, I remember, I heard a sound like crying, in the night. I used to put my head under the blankets when that happened. Now, as I sit here with the old photographs, the feeling I had then comes back to me and I'm close to crying myself. What can it have been like for a woman in the fifties? Mum had a job, in an office somewhere, she never talked about it. She gave it up when she got married. To look after Dad, and then us children. No choice, in those days.

I blow my nose and set to putting the old photographs in order. I'll get one or two framed. I rather like the wedding one with the drooping lilac. Peg can have a look herself and see which ones she'd like. There are some others taken at the factory which I'll let Cecie see, including a nice one of Dad and Madge which she might like. I think old Madge had a soft spot for our Dad, but surely Peg wasn't suggesting that they...? Never!

There's a photograph face down on the floor, must have slipped off the table. I pick it up and turn it over. It's more recent than most of the others. Mum and Dad by the statue of Eric Morecambe. I can't think who would have taken that. I didn't even know they'd been to see the statue. I put that photo on the table alongside the one of them on their wedding day, the one with the lilac. I look at them for quite a time, thinking and wondering, just wondering. Realising how little we know of other people's lives, even our own parents. Perhaps especially our own parents.

# ENVOI

They weren't sure which of them had found out about it, could have been any of the three, Peg, or Dot, or Cecily. But they all applied for tickets and between them they got four, so Cecily said why didn't they invite Madge Turner along, wouldn't it be fun to have a girls' night out together? Madge had been such a stalwart in the factory, and she lived on her own and was probably lonely since she'd retired. Dot said why not? And Peg didn't argue, so Cecily wrote and Madge wrote back right away, a little scented note saying she'd love to go with them to see *Strictly* in Blackpool, thank you so much, it would be a treat, she loved watching it on TV.

It was November, and a chilly night. They had to queue, which was a surprise to them given that they had supposedly been allocated tickets, but actually it was fun. Madge said she was glad of her old red coat with its fur collar, not real fur of course, she assured the others. When they got to the top of the queue, they were given numbers and told what time to come back, so they were off to find a café for fish and chips.

'D'you think Mum and Dad ever did this?' said Peg. 'Went out to a café for a treat?'

Dot shrugged. 'Who knows?' she said. 'I hope so. Everyone deserves a treat now and then.'

When they got back to the Tower Ballroom they had to queue again, and then a third time once they'd given in their coats and bags. Finally they got into their seats, and found they were on the front row.

'Thank goodness we all put our best shoes on,' said Cecily, smiling at the others.

Madge blushed, tucking her feet under her chair. Then she noticed someone waving from the other side of the ballroom, and nudged Cecily.

'Who's that, d'you know them?' she said. But none of them could see properly through the lights, and then the warm-up man was calling for silence and saying they'd be on air in two minutes and he hoped they were all ready with their best claps and cheers. Which of course they were.

*

Across the Ballroom, Vincenzo is in row two, which he's glad about because it's still a good seat and his shoes – which he's forgotten to polish – won't be on display. He was thrilled to get seats, Sandra at the hotel got them and gave them to him so he could take his new boyfriend along, show him off to Henry.

'I can't believe it's five years since I was here last,' he says, looking into his lover's sapphire-blue eyes.

Peering across the expanse of the ballroom he sees some women in the front row on the other side who look familiar. Maybe they've been customers at the hotel, he thinks, but one party merges into another, he can't place them. He waves nonetheless, just in case they recognise him. But before anyone has time to respond there's a call for silence for the start of the show and no one's looking at anyone else in the audience now; all eyes are on the dancers in their sequinned costumes, sparkling under the follow spots.

There's a short break before they film the results show that will be broadcast the following night. The BBC people bring round chocolate bars and cartons of orange juice because they want people to stay in their seats. Later, Vincenzo looks across at the women on the other side of the room again.

In comparison with the dancers they look dowdy, even the one who could be about his age.

'Am I dowdy?' he asks his boyfriend, who merely laughs, tells Vincenzo his English is coming on, and boldly kisses him.

'Ah, young love,' says someone behind them in a loud whisper. They both turn, blushing and pleased to be acknowledged, ignoring a couple of other people who look embarrassed.

When Vincenzo and his lover leave the Tower Ballroom the rain has stopped. They walk a little way and stand and look out across the calm moonlit waters of the bay. Other people are doing the same, taking the night air, Peg and Dot and Cecily and Madge among them. People are smiling at one another.

'Mum and Dad said it was like this just after the war when they first met,' Peg says to her sister. 'People going to dances, forgetting about the rationing, just glad to be able to get out and no more bombs. Though I wouldn't want to go back to that time.'

Peg shivers, just for a moment, hugging herself as the four of them stand there, each thinking her own thoughts. And then they're all off, back into their separate but strangely entwined lives, all having shared something just a little bit magical.

Meeting up that night would have given Cecily the opportunity to give Madge back her lost diary. But she didn't. When she'd asked her husband what she should do, he'd said:

'Keep it. If you give it back it might just open up old wounds for her. And here's another thing. Maybe one day you'll write her story. Change the names though. Make it about another family. Set it in another town, and make it about another industry. That way no one will be hurt, and people may understand a little more about what you said to me. About talking to one another. Put in some other people too, some lighter people, as Shakespeare called them. With a happy love story.'

Cecily thought a lot after that about what she would change and what she wouldn't, if she did decide to write the story of her family. One thing she was sure of: she didn't want to upset anyone, but she would definitely keep all the feelings. All the sadness, and all of the love.

# ACKNOWLEDGEMENTS

Huge thanks to Louise Walters, for taking on the publication of this book and for being both the most meticulous and generous of editors. I could not have asked for better support.

Also to the whole team and fellow authors at Louise Walters Books for welcoming me into the fold.

Thanks also to:

Jane Fraser and Bronwen Griffiths, for always being there at the end of a tweet with writerly support, and to Jackie and Goff Bradshaw, for giving the draft of this novella a sensitivity read for all things Lancastrian.

And, of course, to Oliver and Feely, aka Dude and CatDude, for their constancy.

# LWB INTERVIEWS CATH BARTON...

**When did you decide to become a writer?**
I spent my working life in jobs in which I did a lot of writing on factual subjects, and I always knew I could write proficiently, but I didn't consider writing fiction for a long time because I didn't know what to write about. When we moved to Abergavenny in 2005 my husband joined a taught writing group and when the tutor gave up after a few years, the members continued meeting in one another's houses. I'd been on some interesting journeys abroad and had a yen to write about those, so I asked if I could join. The travel writing didn't come to anything but I felt encouraged in the group to start writing stories. That was about ten years ago. Gradually creative writing became more and more important in my life. Winning the prize for my first novella in 2017 made me feel I could really call myself a writer.

**What kind of books do you enjoy reading?**

I like contemporary fiction. I'm in a couple of reading groups, which throw up titles I wouldn't have considered otherwise, especially historical novels, which I tend to think I'm not going to enjoy and then find I do. An example is Hannah Kent's *Burial Rites,* set in northern Iceland in 1829. I read this several years ago, but the feeling of the story – of a woman condemned to death for her supposed part in the brutal murder of her lover – has stayed with me so strongly. I think that's because of the vivid writing, and also the exploration in the novel of truth and belief. I am drawn to stories about moral complexity. Leila Slimani's *Adèle* is another novel I loved for that reason. It's an exploration of a woman's search for meaning in her life. Both of those books are quite dark. I could go on and on, but I'll just mention one other book I loved, and this one for its quirkiness and its humour, which is Jess Kidd's *Himself.* There are ghosts in this novel, but they are unlike any ghosts you've met before!

**Apart from writing, what are your passions?**

Music is one. I've done a lot of singing, in large and small groups, and some solo singing too. Mostly classical music. I was never as good a singer as I wanted to be, which was frustrating.

Now I mostly listen, and I write reviews of opera and concerts.

I like crafting, though I tend to dabble rather than pursue any one craft seriously. I really enjoy origami – creating a 3-D object from a sheet of paper is very satisfying. I've had a little go at Fair Isle knitting and would love to do more of that. I'm lucky that I live in a place where there are opportunities to learn both of those skills from experts.

Another thing is hill walking. Abergavenny, where I live, is surrounded by beautiful countryside, and I do get out there and up in the hills most weeks. It keeps me fit and gets me away from the computer. It's also the very best thing to counteract the feelings of anxiety which afflict me sometimes.

And I take photographs, which I almost forgot to mention because it's like brushing my teeth, something I do every day without having to put it on my to-do list. I post my photos on a website called Blipfoto. It's a way of keeping a journal and also making friends with people round the world.

**How did you conceive *In the Sweep of the Bay*?**
Like my first novella, *In the Sweep of the Bay* grew from a piece of flash fiction, in this case a story about Ted and Rene, the married couple at the centre of the book, going on an outing. It was about the little

things that go to make up a relationship. From there I worked out and back and around. I tried to create a novella-in-flash, in which each short piece stands alone and together they form more than the sum of the parts. It didn't work in that form, but when I sent an extract to Louise and she said she liked the characters, I started weaving the novella.

**Do you have a favourite among your characters?**
No, not really. I feel for them all. I wonder if, as writers, we put different aspects of ourselves into the characters we write about. It's not something I do consciously, but the unconscious plays a huge role in writing.

**Can you tell us anything about your next project?**
Having always said I'd never write a novel, I did start one during NaNoWriMo (National Novel Writing Month) in 2018. I drafted 50,000 words and put it aside. Then *In the Sweep of the Bay* intervened. I will get back to the novel. It's set in Nepal in the aftermath of an earthquake. It started off as a quest/adventure story, but there's a parallel storyline emerging. Probably best not to say more about that for now – it's still early in the process!

The other big project I have is to write about my Auntie Phyllis, who was an internationally-renowned circus artiste. It can't be a biography because although I have lots of her photographs I have very little written material. So whatever I write will be fictionalised. It feels like something very important for me to write.

And there may be a third novella brewing...

**Who are your favourite writers, and why?**
I love magical realism. So Angela Carter and Gabriel García Márquez are two favourites.

When I was younger I loved Graham Greene's novels. Something about that Catholic angst attracted me. I think actually it's the moral complexity issue that I mentioned earlier. Why people act as they do is something I find endlessly fascinating. Probably that's why I've also enjoyed many of Ian McEwan's novels. Maggie O'Farrell's too.

Then there's poetry. Owen Sheers and Helen Dunmore – two novelists who are also poets. And Dylan Thomas, especially his *Child's Christmas in Wales*. T S Eliot's *Little Gidding*. The sound and rhythm of the words. That's so important to me in the way I write myself, though I don't regard myself as a poet.

**What are the highlights so far of being a published author?**

I've been very touched by the positive comments people have made about my writing. It's very affirming. And I am very happy when readers say that my writing speaks to them. Communicating with others through my writing means a lot to me.

**And what are the lows?**

I have been to some events where only a few people have turned up to hear me. But I know that happens to very famous writers too, so I don't let it get me down. And I've always had a good chat with the few, or once, the only person who came.

**Do you have any advice for readers who are also writers?**

First and foremost, write what you want to write, not what someone else says will sell. Secondly, don't go into writing expecting to make money. Do it because you have something you want to say. Find writerly support, be it through a group or on-line. And develop a thick skin. Your work will be rejected. It doesn't mean that it's worthless. Don't give up. You're the only one who can tell your story. Keep working and keep submitting.

# ALSO FROM
# LOUISE WALTERS BOOKS

Louise Walters Books is the home of intelligent, provocative, beautifully written works of fiction. We are proud of our impressive list of authors and titles. We publish in most genres, but all our titles have one aspect in common: they are brilliantly written.

Further information about all our books and authors can be found on our website:

**louisewaltersbooks.co.uk**

# *Fallible Justice*

## Laura Laakso

*"I am running through the wilderness
and the wilderness runs through me."*

IN OLD LONDON, where
paranormal races co-exist
with ordinary humans,
criminal verdicts delivered
by the all-seeing Heralds
of Justice are infallible. After a man is declared guilty
of murder and sentenced
to death, his daughter
turns to private investiga-
tor Yannia Wilde to do the
impossible and prove the Heralds wrong.

Yannia has escaped a restrictive life in the
Wild Folk conclave where she was raised, but her
origins mark her as an outsider in the city. Those
origins lend her the sensory abilities of all of
nature. Yet Yannia is lonely and struggling to
adapt to life in the city. The case could be the

break she needs. She enlists the help of her only friend, a Bird Shaman named Karrion, and together they accept the challenge of proving a guilty man innocent.

So begins a breathless race against time and against all conceivable odds. Can Yannia and Karrion save a man who has been judged infallibly guilty?

This is fantasy at its most literary, thrilling best, and the first title in Laura's paranormal crime series Wilde Investigations. There is a wonderfully human element to Laura's writing, and her work is fantasy for readers who don't like fantasy (or think they don't!) and perfect, of course, for those who do.

Available in paperback, ebook, and audio.

# *Echo Murder*

## Laura Laakso

*"I'm part of every bird I meet,
and they are all within me."*

YANNIA WILDE RETURNS
to the Wild Folk conclave
where she grew up, and to
the deathbed of her fa-
ther, the conclave's Elderman. She is soon drawn
back into the Wild Folk
way of life and into a tur-
bulent relationship with
Dearon, to whom she is
betrothed.

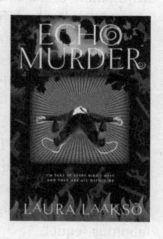

Back in London, unassuming office worker Tim
Wedgebury is surprised when police appear on his
doorstep with a story about how he was stabbed in
the West End. His body disappeared before the
paramedics' eyes. Given that Tim is alive and well,
the police chalk the first death up to a Mage prank.
But when Tim "dies" a second time, Detective

Inspector Jamie Manning calls Yannia and, torn between returning to the life she has built in Old London and remaining loyal to the conclave and to Dearon, she strikes a compromise with the Elderman that allows her to return temporarily to the city.

There she sets about solving the mystery of Tim's many deaths with the help of her apprentice, Karrion. They come to realise that with every death, more of the echo becomes reality, and Yannia and Karrion find themselves in increasing danger as they try to save Tim. Who is the echo murderer? What sinister game are they playing? And what do they truly want?

The second of Laura Laakso's Wilde Investigations series reveals more of her wonderful characters and their complexities and struggles, both personal and professional. The crucial human element that sets Laura's work apart really comes to the fore in this fabulous sequel.

Available in paperback, ebook, and audio.

# *Roots of Corruption*

### Laura Laakso

*"What could Lady Bergamon have to fear
in a garden of her own making?"*

ON THE NIGHT of Samhain, the veil between worlds is at its thinnest, and ancient magic runs wild in Old London.

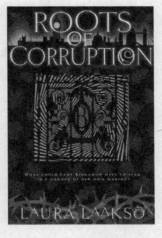

When Lady Bergamon is attacked in her Ivy Street garden, Wishearth turns to Yannia for help. Who could have the power to harm Lady Bergamon in her own domain? While Yannia searches for the answer, nature herself appears to be killing Mages in Old London. Yannia and Karrion join forces with New Scotland Yard to solve the baffling Mage deaths. But wherever they turn, all the clues point back towards Ivy Street.

Yannia's abilities are put to the test as she races to save Lady Bergamon's life, and prevent further murders. But with the lines between friends and enemies blurring, she must decide who to trust and how much she's willing to sacrifice for Old London and its inhabitants...

The third of Laura Laakso's Wilde Investigations series continues the tale of Yannia, Karrion, Lady Bergamon, Wishearth, et al. A wonderful novel that sees the series step up a gear; and gives readers a glimpse of the epic battles to come. Brilliant stuff!

Available in paperback, ebook, and audio.

# The Last Words of Madeleine Anderson

## Helen Kitson

*"Writing is like a love affair, or should be. You get to know your story, it intrigues you, if you're lucky it enthrals you, and ultimately it ends, leaving you wretched and abandoned."*

ONCE UPON A TIME Gabrielle Price wrote and published an extraordinary novel.

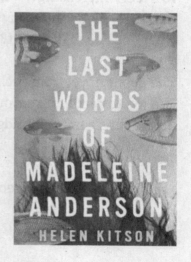

But twenty years on her literary star has dimmed, her "work of genius" is all but forgotten, and no further novels have materialized. She now lives an unremarkable life: middle-aged, living alone in the sleepy village she grew up in, and working as a housekeeper for the local vicar. Her lonely existence is dominated by memories of her best friend Madeleine, who died young, in tragic and mysterious circumstances.

Gabrielle's quiet world is turned upside down when she meets and befriends Simon – young, attractive, a would-be writer, and enthusiastic fan of the astonishing novel that Gabrielle published all those years ago. Charmed and flattered, she recklessly invites him into her home and her heart. But Simon is mysterious and manipulative, and it's not long before he forces Gabrielle to confront the demons in her past. Gabrielle's obsession begins to destroy her carefully cultivated life, and she comes to feel increasingly threatened by Simon's presence. Who is he? Why did he seek her out? And what does he really want?

The debut novel from acclaimed poet Helen Kitson is a joy to read: mysterious, reflective, and darkly humorous. Diana Cambridge describes it as "Barbara Pym noir".

Available in paperback, ebook, and audio.

# Don't Think a Single Thought

## Diana Cambridge

*"Hello? Hello? Emma, is that you? Emma! It's only
me... Hello? Are you there, Emma?"*

1960S NEW YORK: Emma
Bowden seems to have it all
– a glamorous Manhattan
apartment, a loving hus-
band, a successful writing
career. But while on vaca-
tion at the Hamptons, a
child drowns in the sea, and
suspicion falls on Emma.
As her picture-perfect life
spirals out of control, old

wounds resurface, dark secrets are revealed, and
that persistent voice in Emma's head that won't
leave her alone threatens to destroy all that Emma
has worked for...

Taut, mesmerising and atmospheric, *Don't Think a
Single Thought* is a novel of dreams and nightmares,

joy and despair, love and hate. It lays bare a marriage, and a woman, and examines the decisions – and mistakes – which shape all of our lives.

Diana Cambridge's debut novel is beautifully written, and tackles big themes in few words. Sophisticated and refreshingly short, this is the perfect holiday or handbag book.

Available in paperback, ebook, and audio.

# The Naseby Horses

## Dominic Brownlow

*'I only know Charlotte is not dead. I feel it within me, her heartbeat the echo of my own. She is with me still. She is near. I have to save her, for that is all in life I have ever been required to do.'*

SEVENTEEN-YEAR-OLD Simon's sister Charlotte is missing. The lonely Fenland village the family recently moved to from London is odd, silent, and mysterious. Simon is epileptic and his seizures are increasing in severity, but when he discovers the local curse of the Naseby

Horses, he is convinced it has something to do with Charlotte's disappearance. Despite resistance from the villagers, the police, and his own family, Simon is determined to uncover the truth behind the curse, and rescue his sister.

Under the oppressive Fenland skies and in the heat of a relentless June, Simon's bond with Charlotte is fierce, all-consuming, and unbreakable; but can he save his adored sister? And does she want to be saved?

Drawing on philosophy, science, and the natural world, *The Naseby Horses* is a moving exploration of the bond between a brother and his sister; of love; and of the meaning of life itself.

Literary, but gripping and readable, this was the first Louise Walters Books hardback.

Available in hardback, paperback, and ebook

**Louise Walters Books extends its gratitude to our Supporters. Supporter subscriptions are invaluable to a small publisher like us.**

Please visit louisewaltersbooks/lwb-supporters if you would like to receive a year's worth of books, invitations to launch parties, exclusive newsletters, early glimpses of forthcoming covers, and many other nice bookish things.

### Heartfelt thanks to:

Claire Allen
Edie Anderson
Karen Ankers
Francesca Bailey-Karel
Tricia Beckett
JEJ Bray
Melanie Brennan
Tom & Sue Carmichael
Liz Carr
Penny Carter-Francis
Pippa Chappell
Eric Clarke
Karen Cocking
Louise Cook
Deborah Cooper
Tina deBellegarde
Giselle Delsol
James Downs

Jill Doyle
Kathryn Eastman
Rowena Fishwick
Harriet Freeman
Diane Gardner
Ian Hagues
Andrea Harman
Stephanie Heimer
Debra Hills
Henrike Hirsch
Claire Hitch
Amanda Huggins
Cath Humphris
Christine Ince
Julie Irwin
Merith Jones
Seamus Keaveny
Moon Kestrel

Ania Kierczyńska
Michael Lynes
Karen Mace
Marie-Anne Mancio
Karen May
Cheryl Mayo
Jennifer McNicol
MoMoBookDiary
Rosemary Morgan
Jackie Morrison
Louise Mumford
Trevor Newton
Aveline Perez de Vera
Mary Picken
Helen Poore
Helen Poyer

Clare Rhoden
Gillian Stern
John Taylor
Julie Teckman
Sarah Thomas
Sue Thomas
Mark Thornton
Penny Tofiluk
Mary Turner
Ian Walters
Steve Walters
Elizabeth Waugh
Alexis Wolfe
Finola Woodhouse
Louise Wykes